TRIAL

BY

FIRE

An End-Times Thriller Novel

By Patience Prence

Spring Harvest
UNITED STATES OF AMERICA

TRIAL BY FIRE

By Patience Prence

www.thespringharvest.com

All Scripture quotations are taken from the King James Version of the Bible.

Published by
Spring Harvest U.S.A.
Copyright © 2015 by Patience Prence
All rights reserved.
ISBN-978-0-9826336-2-5

Books by
Patience Prence

SCARS: An Amazing End-Times Prophecy Novel

TRIAL BY FIRE: An End-Times Thriller Novel

*For Yeshua, my Guiding Light, and
to all the fans of SCARS.*

ACKNOWLEDGMENTS

It is with great joy that I honor the people who helped and believed in me throughout this amazing journey. First and foremost, this novel would not have come into existence if not for the fans of SCARS who encouraged and inspired me to keep writing. I was not planning to write another book. Thank you for your kind letters and reviews and asking for more.

\#

And a big thanks to my loving husband, Dennis, for standing beside me and for his unwavering support and ideas. He is my rock!

Thank you from the bottom of my heart to my mother. Words cannot express my gratitude to her for listening and critiquing as I read to her one chapter at a time.

A special thanks to those who helped make Trial by Fire a reality: Debbie Cole, editor; Ray Sorensen, contributing editor; Ed Gardner, cover designer.

Last but not least, I want to express my immense love and gratitude to my family: Dennis, Mom, Dad, Imelda, Nancy, Janet, James and Maria, I love you all. James, let me know when you see this; I'll know you read the book!

That the trial of your faith, being much more precious than of gold that perisheth, though it be tried with fire, might be found unto praise and honour and glory at the appearing of Jesus Christ.

1 Peter 1:7

CHAPTER

1

If ye were of the world, the world would love his own: but because ye are not of the world, but I have chosen you out of the world, therefore the world hateth you. Remember the word that I said unto you, The servant is not greater than his lord. If they have persecuted me, they will also persecute you; if they have kept my saying, they will keep yours also. But all these things will they do unto you for my name's sake, because they know not him that sent me.
John 15:19-21

"Behold, the head of a resister!" The executioner holds his trophy high above for all to see.

Brock Summers trembles with fear. He doesn't want to acknowledge what just happened—although he knows it did. He tries to detach himself from this horrific nightmare.

Death lingers in the air. A large blue-and-white flag, its ten stars symbolizing the ten World Unions, sways sluggishly as violet and scarlet streaks of light fade.

Great numbers of people have massed below the metal-and-glass building that penetrates the skyline. Many came early, vying for the best location from which to observe this grisly form of entertainment.

Boots trample heavily on the ground as two black-hooded men walk toward the line of prisoners.

Brock inhales deeply. Who will be next?

His throat constricts. He feels as if he is being choked to death.

The hooded men reach the prisoners.

Brock holds his breath.

They move past him. They stop before a heavy-set, African American woman; her short nappy hair frames her round face. Her eyebrows are furrowed together, the corners of her lips turned down and her chin pushed up.

An invisible weight presses hard against Brock's chest. He recognizes the woman as the one who sat next to Becky at his trial.

The thought of Becky stirs emotions deep inside his core. He brings up an image of her sitting in the back row of the courtroom; she is so young and innocent, her blond hair tied back into a ponytail.

Although they'd only met briefly in their box-car prison, he thought of her like a little sister.

Where is she? he agonizes. He didn't see her when he came to the courtyard. Was she released? Did her mother come and get her? Her words ring in his head. *"I will never worship Maitreyas. I'd rather die than worship him!"*

Was she executed? Quickly he ejects the ghastly thought from his head.

"Prisoner 2-8-5-0-9-9."

"Yes, sir." The black woman acknowledges the number as her own.

A gloved hand grips her elbow. "Come with us." The masked man yanks her forward.

The woman glares into the round eyeholes of the mask. "I knows my way, suh." She pulls her arm back. "I'se going to see my Lord Jesus, just like de saints before me."

"Hey, stupid!" A man with a swastika tattooed on his forehead grins. "Everybody knows Jesus is in Rome. You're dying for a lost cause—a figment of your imagination." The man glances toward two young girls who smile and laugh with approval.

"Yeah!" another man shouts. "Peter Roma—Petrus Romanus, he is in Rome!"

Ignoring the insults, the woman begins walking forward, an executioner on each side of her. The legs of her orange jumpsuit rub together, and the metal chains on her ankles clink. A small step follows another then another. She lifts her sandaled foot off the pavement and steps onto the dead grass. Holding her head high and her shoulders back, she makes her way toward the bloodthirsty beast that sits in the middle of the courtyard, its metal blade beckoning its next victim.

How brave she is, Brock thinks. *If she's afraid she doesn't show it.*

"PE-TER, PE-TER, PE-TER." A shirtless man wearing cutoff jeans and a full body tattoo of a cobra begins chanting and clapping trying to rouse the crowd. His stomach is yellow, and olive-green scales with yellow cross bands run down the length of his back and down his legs.

Brock's nose wrinkles in disgust when he notices the man's tongue has been surgically modified and is forked like a snake. *What a freak.*

With his hands cuffed in front of him Brock brushes the trickle of sweat off his brow with his arm. His face is rugged and pleasing in appearance with a strong, wide jaw and straight nose. His once professionally styled wavy, black hair is now matted and mingled with sweat. The orange uniform shows off his strong physique from the countless hours of working out.

"PE-TER, PE-TER, PE-TER." People wave small World Union flags and hold handmade posters and signs.

A black-haired, gothic-style girl waves a poster high

over her head: "Behead those who insult Lord Maitreyas."

"PE-TER, PE-TER, PE-TER...."

Peter Roma. Brock recalls the man who fulfilled Saint Malachy's prophecy, the man who would reign and feed his flock until the seven-hilled city would be destroyed.

He reflects on how shocked and appalled he was when Peter Roma announced to the world that he was "Jesus, but not the Christ," that he'd come to prepare the way for the Christ. He claimed that he'd ascended with a new body, therefore erasing his scars from his death and resurrection, and was in his final incarnation as Petrus Romanus—the master of wisdom.

"That's Lorraine." A prisoner interrupts Brock's thoughts. "She didn't say one word at her trial."

Brock turns toward the man; his tawny-blond hair is woven with gray and pulled back into a ponytail. He looks familiar, but Brock can't place him.

"Oh," Brock replies in a sullen, monotone voice.

"All she did was sit there and look at the prosecutor with a blank stare. The judge was so irritated with her, he told her she would waste no more of the court's time and sentenced her to death by decapitation."

"I'm so sorry for her." Brock tightens his lips and shakes his head.

"By the way," the man says, extending his shackled hand, "my name is Jesse."

Brock notices a red, jagged scar above Jesse's brow as he accepts his friendly grip.

"I'm Brock."

"Yes, I know."

An uncomfortable feeling sweeps over Brock. He wonders if Jesse witnessed his humiliating court trial or if he knew him from reporting the news.

At thirty-three years old, Brock Summers was one of

the top reporters at Channel 13 news in Los Angeles, California, the affiliate station of WNN (World News Network).

Since his early teens, Brock loved to write and was hooked on the news, reading blogs and watching reports from around the world. With much encouragement from his aunt Millie, he decided to go into journalism after watching a film about two reporters who broke the biggest story of the 1970s—the Watergate scandal. It was originally a small story, but because these two men pursued the facts it brought down a president. That was a huge accomplishment in Brock's eyes, stirring within him the desire to find the facts and expose them through investigative journalism.

After a few years of college Brock worked as a writer, then a radio reporter and later an intern at a news station. One day they were shorthanded and needed someone to do a simple interview. Brock jumped at the chance.

After the interview dozens of female fans wrote into the studio demanding more of Brock. His charm and good looks helped win over the female producer who found him a permanent position reporting the news.

Brock's chestnut-brown eyes wander to the black print on the back of a kid's T-shirt: *"RESISTERS WANTED: DEAD OR ALIVE."*

The chanting diminishes, and people begin whispering and talking to each other, keeping their eyes on Lorraine.

A small sparrow hawk drops from the sky and lands on the upraised hand of the gold Maitreyas statue that sits across from the guillotine. An aura of glamour and mystery envelops the bird. He puffs out his orange-striped chest and gazes down toward Lorraine as though he were a Roman emperor being entertained by the persecution of the Christians.

Brock looks at Lorraine's bracelet and then unconsciously at his own; it is green and the size of a diver's watch. It displays a six-digit identification number and a barcode.

His eyes move to the crack in the concrete.

I can't believe they are going to behead this woman, he mutters to himself. *I just can't believe it.*

> I' be trav'lin' in de footsteps
>> Of those who've gone before—

Brock looks up.

> And I' be re-united
>> On a new and sunlit shore. . . .

He scans the crowd to see where the outburst of singing is coming from. He settles on the large, orange jumpsuit in the middle of the courtyard. It is Lorraine. A small smile forms on his lips.

> Oh, when de saints,
>> go marchin' in,
> Oh, when de saints
>> go marchin' in. . . .

Her multi-octave voice has that old-time gospel energy that commands attention; it is ineffable.

> Lord, Lord, I'se gonna be in dat number,
>> when de saints go marchin' in. . . .

"Praise Jesus!" shouts a giant, bald, African American prisoner. "Glory, glory to Jesus!"

6

As Lorraine sings, her cuffed hands fold together and press against her chest; her face tilts upward, and her eyes look up toward heaven.

> An when de sun refuse to shine,
>> An when de sun refuse to shine,
> Lord, Lord, I'se gonna be in dat number,
>> When de sun refuse to shine. . . .

Brock recognizes the tune but realizes Lorraine is singing her own version. He feels her heartfelt emotion as she pours out her soul.

"DEATH TO THE RESISTER!" a man shouts, and a brown shoe sails past Lorraine's head and hits one of the executioners.

The executioner stops and turns around to see a World Union guard wrestling the perpetrator to the ground. The executioner turns back and resumes his position next to Lorraine.

Lorraine continues to produce melodious sounds as the trio moves closer to the guillotine.

> An when de moon turns red with blood,
>> An when de moon turns red with blood,
> Lord, I'se gonna be in dat number,
>> When the moon turns red with blood—

Lorraine stops singing. She has reached the end of her journey.

Silence.

One of the executioners grabs Lorraine's elbow while the other one turns his back and stands at attention at the base of the steps.

A black-hooded man stands nearby with a

wheelbarrow loaded with sand, and another stands at the base of the scaffold near an empty bucket and gaping wood box that sits ready to swallow up the remains.

Brock's heart rate accelerates.

Lorraine glances up at the instrument of her execution, a giant metal blade rising to the sky. She submits with composure and grace and turns toward the executioner. "I am ready to meet my Lord."

Lifting her foot, the pair begins their ascent up the splintered stairs. She struggles to climb the first two steps and leans her weight on the executioner and concentrates all her effort to lift her foot.

She stops for a minute to catch her breath. Slowly she begins climbing again. Step after step, step after step.

They reach the landing and move toward the wood frame.

The executioner holds Lorraine's elbow as she bends her knees and lowers herself to the floor. A small grunt escapes her lips when her knees hit the rough wood. Leaning forward Lorraine places her head into the open lunette and closes her eyes.

Brock notices her lips are moving. *She is praying.* He shakes involuntarily and labors to catch his breath. Shifting from one leg to the other, he feels a sudden surge of inner torment.

Turning away, he glances at the spectators. Excitement is written all over their faces as they stretch their necks hoping to catch a glimpse of the gory spectacle.

The silence is foreboding.

Brock fights the impulse to vomit. Squeezing his eyes shut he draws in a deep breath and tries to focus on anything but what is about to happen. But he keeps visualizing Lorraine up there kneeling, ready to join the saints, just like the song she sang; any moment now and it will all be over.

There is a thunderous rolling sound like metal grinding wood.

Brock's body stiffens; he doesn't breathe.

A quick crashing bang is accompanied by loud screams and gasps from the crowd.

Brock feels his legs buckle. He fights back tears.

"It's over." Jesse brushes the wet streaming from his own eyes. "Lorraine is with Jesus now."

"Behold, the head of a resister!" an executioner shouts over the crowd. "Long live Lord Maitreyas!"

Spectators cheer in jubilee. "Hail, Lord Maitreyas!"

Tears gush forth. *Get ahold of yourself, man,* Brock scolds himself. It takes every ounce of will power to get a grip on his emotions. Taking the back of his hand he wipes the burning moisture from his eyes and does his best to compose himself.

The sparrow hawk emits a piercing screech as it flies away.

The two executioners walk back down the path and veer left then walk up the steps of the building. They disappear behind the double-glass doors.

Is it over? Brock wonders.

"Mr. Summers! Mr. Summers!"

Brock looks up to see a skinny, red-headed man working his way through the crowd toward him. His right hand clutches a camera that hangs around his neck.

"Hi, Mr. Summers!" His cheeks are covered with freckles. "My name is Bob Brown, and I'm with the *North American Times.* May I ask you a few questions?" Bob pulls a pen and pad of paper out of the pocket of his blue jeans.

You idiot! Brock wants to yell at the man. *Can't you see someone just died? Have you no respect?* Instead he tries to brush him off. "I don't think now is a good time." His voice is cold. He looks past the reporter to the guillotine.

"Yes, I know. . .but only a few questions, Mr. Summers?"

Brock sees two men loading Lorraine's remains into a cart, and then he turns his attention back to the reporter.

Brock hesitates. As a reporter he knows this man will not leave until he gets what he's looking for—a story.

"I guess. . .but only a few questions."

Pen in hand Bob asks, "How do you feel about people being executed?"

"I am disgusted beyond words."

Bob scribbles away on his note pad then looks up.

"Brock, you are a famous news reporter. Was it worth it to jeopardize your career and possibly lose your life just for a story?"

"When I decided to go into journalism my goal was to expose the truth. And that's what I did— expose the truth."

Bob writes some more.

Brock turns his eyes to the hooded man standing by the guillotine near the wheelbarrow. He watches him shovel sand onto the crimson platform.

"What was prison like. . .were you treated well?"

Brock's mind goes back to his tiny isolated cell where he thought he would die of insanity. He looks directly into the reporter's freckled face. "If you think I had any special treatment, you are wrong. I was treated just like any other prisoner."

"Oh, sorry, Mr. Summers. I wasn't implying anything, really. Okay, now I understand you will be pardoned under certain conditions. Have you met those conditions and taken the oath?"

"I—"

"HEY! HEY, YOU THERE!" An angry voice shouts above the crowd.

Brock turns to see a World Union guard in a tan

uniform and blue beret pointing at Bob Brown.

"NO TALKING TO THE PRISONERS!"

"Sorry, sir." With a satisfied look on his face the reporter turns and vanishes into the mob of people.

The guard shakes his head and mumbles something about the stupid media and walks back to his post at the top of the steps of the courthouse.

With dismay in their eyes, the prisoners stand still while the people whisper and point at them. They look up when the glass doors swing open and out walk the two executioners. They stop and talk with the World Union guard, the same one who scolded Bob Brown.

The guard looks down as he flips through the papers on his clipboard. He points to a paper. One of the executioners nods.

Brock relives the horror he felt earlier as the two executioners shuffle toward him and the other prisoners.

He holds his breath. *Did the judge change his mind? Are they going to execute me anyway?*

They pass him and stop in front of a young Italian man in his late teens. He has long black hair and a scruffy beard, and his nose reminds Brock of a parrot's beak.

"Prisoner 2-7-9-4-5-2."

The Italian's brows shoot up. "NO! NO!" he shrieks.

"Come with us." An executioner grabs his elbow and pulls him out of the line.

The Italian pulls away and drops to his knees. "I can't do it. . .I just can't go through with it." His head falls between his knees, and he sobs uncontrollably.

A man mocks. "Hey! Where's your faith now, skinny runt? Ha ha ha! What a pathetic coward."

"Yeah, you're a yellow belly—your belly is as yellow as the snake man's belly!" another man jeers.

The snake man raises his hands high over his head

and starts clapping and rotating his hips. "Yellow belly, yellow belly, I'm a yellow belly!" People laugh and clap. The snake man sticks out his split tongue and wiggles it up and down.

The executioner tugs at the Italian's elbows. "Come on, young man. Get up! Don't make me drag you."

"Be strong, brother," Jesse tells the young man. "You can do it—fear not the one who can destroy your body, but fear the one who can destroy both your body and soul in hell."

The young Italian continues to sob, not budging.

The executioner stands and yells toward the glass doors. "Guard! Over here!"

Clutching his clipboard, the guard takes big strides through the people.

His hands on his hips, the executioner laughs. "Looks like this one may not be so eager to meet his lord like that last lady."

"What is your name, young man?" The guard directs his question at the pile of orange rags crumpled on the ground.

"Art. . .Arturo Corelli."

"Arturo, did you know the World Union constitution has a clause that allows any resister who takes the oath and bows down to Lord Maitreyas's statue to be pardoned?"

"Uh. . .no." He sniffles.

Brock recalls when Peter Roma introduced the oath. "No one will enter the Age of Aquarius unless he takes the Luciferian initiation. After the initiation into the secret doctrines your third eye will be opened, and you will have access to communicate with the powers."

"Arturo, will you take the oath?"

"No! Don't do it, Arturo!" pleads the seven-foot black man. "Your soul will be tormented in hell."

"Your soul will be tormented in hell" reverberates through Brock's mind as though the words were meant for him. The gavel of shame slams hard against his guilty chest.

"Be strong, Arturo. You can do it. . . ." The African American continues to encourage the young Italian.

"Shut up, black fool," a male voice calls out.

Arturo lifts his head slowly. "I—I dunno."

"Come on, Arturo. Let's go NOW!" The executioner grabs his arm and starts dragging him down the sidewalk toward the guillotine.

"Okay!" he bellows. "Okay, I will take the oath—"

"Escort the prisoner back in line, corporal."

"Yes, sir!"

CHAPTER

2

The long bus ride back to prison doesn't calm Brock's nerves; he is exhausted and emotionally drained. He shifts on the rock-hard seat, his six-feet-four-inch height crammed in the upright coffin space at the back of the bus.

All is quiet except for road noise, snoring and an occasional cough. His head rests against the vibrating glass window covered with bars. Among the twenty or so inmates, he recognizes some who stood with him during the executions, but he doesn't know why the others are there.

His eyes close, and he tries to block the horrific events of the day. But he can't keep from grieving from all he has witnessed and endured.

The sweat box jerks when it hits a pothole in the road.

He rebels at the idea of returning to his cell. After they arrested him they put him in isolation. His space was so small that he could stand in one place and touch both walls at the same time and reach up and touch the fluorescent lights on the ceiling that hummed constantly, driving him crazy. His bed almost filled the entire room with just enough space for a sink and a toilet. Ants and cockroaches shared his cube and even a brown mouse. He was so lonely at times he would purposely leave crumbs in hopes that "Mickey" would visit and entertain him.

The worst part of his tiny cell was no windows, just four walls of peeling gray paint. He never knew if it was day or night. He would fall asleep and wake up not knowing if it was the next day or just a few hours later so he began counting food trays to keep track of time. Sometimes, though, he was sure the guards forgot about him, and he feared he would starve to death.

With no air conditioning the heat was at times so unbearable he would stop up the sink with his clothes and let the water pour out onto the floor. He would then lie naked on the wet ground to keep cool.

The guards who brought his meals were the only humans he ever saw except for the inmates he showered with once a week.

He had no visitors, no recreation, no TV or any reading material except for "The New Gospel" and a writing tablet and pen.

To keep sane, he would fold up his bed on its side and work out by doing push ups and sit ups and run in place. Sometimes he would shut his eyes and visualize he was jogging along the beach.

The bus slows then lurches as it turns right. The driver maneuvers into an asphalt lot surrounded by two rows of chain link fence topped by razor-sharp barbed wire. An automatic gate opens, and a guard waves at the driver. They pass through the second gate and enter the compound. The bus grinds to a halt in a large parking lot filled with police and World Union vehicles. The prisoners stand and stretch then exit single file and are directed to different areas of a large, gray-brick building where each prisoner is processed.

After his paperwork is finished Brock follows the khaki-colored uniform down the narrow corridor. He glances at the black service belt weighted down by a baton, pepper spray, handcuffs, keys and a gas mask.

They end up in a room where he strips out of his jumpsuit and is uncomfortably searched.

The guard removes his metal restraints. "Move forward," he says in a gruff tone.

Naked and covering his private parts with his tennis

shoes, Brock steps ahead of the guard. They walk down a narrow hall into a room where a small table stands and shelves are lined with neatly folded, stained white towels.

Brock helps himself to the items on the table.

"Ten minutes," the guard says, swinging the metal door open.

The smell of urine, mold and disinfectant blasts Brock's nostrils as he steps inside the small room. He hears the click of the door shutting behind him. The sound of water splashing on the floor and gurgling down the drain signals he is not alone. His eyes fasten on the silhouette of a tall black figure illuminated by a single light bulb fixture hanging from the ceiling.

Clutching a bar of soap and disposable razor he moves across the chipped, cracked white tile keeping his eye on the tall figure.

His fingers turn the single-handled faucet until cold liquid spurts from the shower head and gushes down his shoulders and back.

Squeezing his eyes shut he dips his head under the stream and lathers his body with soap. With a steady hand he begins shaving the hair off his face, removing all traces of his beard.

Tap, tap, tap. The guard strikes the metal door with a baton. "Cornelius, time's up."

The handle across the room creaks, and the flow of water stops. The giant man steps away from the shower and glances over at Brock. "Good evening, sir!" he says then exits the shower room.

Brock recognizes him—Cornelius, the bald, black man who was at the execution encouraging the young Italian Arturo.

****

With a blanket tucked under his arm and wearing clean, orange scrubs Brock follows the guard down the hallway. He is relieved to discover they are not going to his old cell.

He hears a clicking sound.

The guard retrieves the plastic card he'd inserted into the slot.

Metal groans and squeaks as the barred door rolls open.

Brock steps into a nine-foot-by-twelve-foot cell.

A whirring fixture overhead floods the small space with light.

The door slides behind him, and the guard vanishes down the hall.

He gazes over the small space: two white plastic chairs on the right, in front of a grungy wall of peeling paint; steel bunks on the left; a steel toilet and sink on the back wall below a long, narrow window.

A foul odor assaults his nose; apparently flushing was not a priority of the previous inmate.

Holding his breath he walks over and pushes the toilet handle, and the contents swirl and disappear.

Not bothering to remove his shoes, he collapses onto the lower bunk; his head sinks into the pillow, and his lids close instantly.

His brain replays the court scene as if it were recorded on a DVR player. He sees himself sitting in the metal chair near the judge; all eyes are on him.

Before he came to trial, he was somewhat optimistic. How could they prove *Wake Up, America!* was his newspaper? He'd covered all his tracks, or so he'd thought.

The recorder in his mind plays the audio sound of the

prosecutor speaking down to him. *"You know, Brock, owning and/or distributing anti-World Union propaganda breaks the law and is punishable by death, and the evidence brought before this court is piled a mile high against you!"*

How was he supposed to know every printer printed an invisible code? If he'd only known he would have paid cash for his computer and had his paper printed on a public copier; then they would never have traced it back to him. *Who knew?*

The prosecutor's words continue to play. *"It would be such a waste for a talented young reporter like you to throw his life away for such hateful and ridiculous lies. I don't want to see you die, the judge does not want to see you die, and Lord Maitreyas does not want to see you die. Brock, do you want to die?*

"Let Lord Maitreyas—the Christ—spare your life, Brock. All you have to do is believe in him and take his mark as a symbol of your loyalty!"

Two sets of footsteps coming down the corridor interrupt Brock's thoughts.

The steps stop at the cell door.

Click.

Opening his eyes Brock rolls over to his side and props his head up with his pillow. Raising his hand to block the glare from the light he watches the door slide open.

In walks a tall, thin-shouldered body silhouetted against the light. Brock recognizes the scar over the brow of the man's wrinkled face and his blond-gray ponytail.

"Hey!" Brock's voice is friendly.

"Hey!" Jesse's bloodshot eyes greet his in recognition.

Quietly Jesse moves across the floor toward the beds. He tosses his folded blanket on the top bunk then hoists himself up.

After a few minutes Brock hears one plop then

another as two tennis shoes fall to the ground. The steel bed makes a series of sharp, grating sounds then stills.

Brock settles down again and rolls toward the wall. To escape this terrifying nightmare he closes his eyes again and tries to sleep.

An evil presence snakes its way around his body like an iron chain as heaviness submerges itself onto his chest. It feels as if it is squeezing the life out of his hollow empty shell. He forces himself to breathe as it moves like a python and compresses his windpipe.

"You shall burn for your betrayal! You will be tortured in the flame!" a sinister voice snickers in his head. *"Feel the pain, feel the hate, feel the flame at hell's gate!"*

An excruciating pain stabs him, like claws cutting into his brain. *"Surrender yourself, you puny mortal."*

NOOO! Brock screams in his head. *Go away. . .leave me alone!*

"I will never leave! I have authority over you, for you have rejected the worthless and vile Son. You are mine for eternity."

The joy Brock once knew has fled, and darkness takes its place. He feels dead inside. He pulls his brown blanket like grave dirt over his face; he buries himself in his tomb of shame and hopelessness.

CHAPTER

3

But whom say ye that I am? And Simon Peter answered and said, Thou art the Christ, the Son of the living God. And Jesus answered and said unto him, Blessed art thou, Simon Barjona: for flesh and blood hath not revealed it unto thee, but my Father which is in heaven.
Matthew 16:15-17

Trembling, Brock sits up in bed. Did he yell out loud—or imagine it? Did he wake up Jesse?

He listens.

An entire ten minutes pass without any sound except for the humming of the light fixture.

Just a bad dream.

Tense muscles soon relax, and his mind slips back into a dream consciousness playing intense, sensorimotor hallucination. . . .

The creaking noise of the upper bunk pulls him out of another deep sleep.

He blinks several times, his eyes adjusting to the light. He forces the fog from his head, and his thoughts clear—he's in jail.

He props himself on his elbows and turns his head slowly toward the slit window.

Feeble gleams of light pour through the glass and into

the cell, exposing things hidden in the shadows the night before. Yellow crud hugs the base of the toilet, and purple mold crawls along the water pipe then vanishes behind the wall. A crack darts across the ceiling. An earthquake?

A flash of orange material is followed by a dull thump as bare feet hit the concrete floor.

"Morning." Jesse stretches his arms to the ceiling.

"Morning," Brock replies.

Jesse walks over to the toilet.

Brock turns his head and rests it back on the pillow. He stares up at the bottom of the blue mattress.

The toilet flushes.

"I wonder what's for breakfast." Jesse rubs his hands under the stream of liquid flowing through the sink faucet.

"Don't know." Brock feels his stomach fuss.

Jesse turns off the handle and wipes his hands on his pant leg.

"How'd you sleep?"

"Lousy, I had a bad dream then woke up with a splitting headache."

"Too bad." Jesse leans against the ledge and gazes out the window.

"Yeah."

Sounds fill the air as prisoners wake up. Men shout back and forth while others yell and bang on the iron bars. The boisterous noise grates on Brock's nerves; it reminds him of an insane asylum.

Tuning out the noise, he recalls the execution.

A deep sadness fills him as he pictures Lorraine stepping onto the platform then dropping to her knees and placing her head inside the open lunette.

His mind backpedals to his trial; he sees the prosecutor bearing down on him. "That's why you get only this one chance, Brock. Accept Maitreyas as your lord and savior. Take his mark. Or be put to death—"

"And when the saints go marching in. . . ." A man's voice harmonizes from across the hall.

Brock stops and listens to the low baritone voice. It is soothing to his ears.

"And when the saints go—"

"DON'T YOU IDIOTS EVER SHUT UP?" a raucous voice with a Hispanic accent hollers from the cell next door.

The singing stops.

Jesse moves away from the window and walks toward the front of the cell; Brock rolls off his cot and follows him. A screwdriver pain jabs behind his eye reminding him of his headache.

Brock recognizes the Italian standing in the cell catty-cornered from theirs.

"Who're you calling an idiot?" Arturo glares straight ahead, his face tight.

"You and all you Christian fundamentists are idiots, that's who!" replies the Hispanic voice.

"It's okay, Arturo. I'll stop singing," says a deep voice from the back of Arturo's cell.

"Hey, aren't you the yellow belly?" asks the Hispanic. "Professor, come and look—it's the coward yellow belly from the execution! Ha ha ha!"

Arturo's face becomes beet red, and his veins pop out on his neck. "If these bars weren't here I'd smash in your face!"

"Now isn't that loving of you?" the Hispanic replies sarcastically. "You're gonna smash my face in. Ha! I thought your god told you to love? Such a hypocrite! Ha, ha. All fundys are hypocrites, eh, professor?"

"Yes, Mario," a nasally voice replies. "Believers have a peculiar habit of professing beliefs they do not exercise."

"Yeah," agrees the one called Mario. "They say one

thing and do another. . .they don't practice what they preach. . .they talk the talk, but they don't walk the walk." A black man appears and stands next to Arturo. Brock recognizes him as the one from the execution, the one the guard called Cornelius.

"Mario, you are right. We are to love one another as Jesus loved us. He loved us so much that He laid His life down for us and He's returning real soon to take us home."

"Blah blah blah. You fundys are a bunch of crazy lunatics!"

"I'm sorry you feel that way, Mario. For some reason, you seem to be very angry at believers. Why would you care if some of us have peace through our Lord Jesus Christ?"

"Don't bother with him, Mario."

That sounds like the professor.

"Just because Peter Roma doesn't have holes in his hands and didn't return in the way they expected, these guys are staunch in believing an imaginary sky fairy is coming back to save them."

Brock pictures the professor looking like his nerdy teacher in college—a middle-aged man with black hair and black-rimmed glasses.

"They're in the same realm as those who believed the earth was flat until they were proved wrong. They believe in ghosts and goblins and even Santa Claus and the Easter bunny. They live their lives based on these fictional characters created in their minds, so why bother with them? Let them enjoy their comfortable club membership and their empty platitudes."

"Uh, excuse me, professor," says Cornelius, "but Peter Roma is *not* Jesus. Jesus was kind and loving, and His message was to love one another. Peter Roma is a war-mongering, hate-filled beast. The fact that he is persecuting the resisters of the World Union and sending them to their deaths 'proves' he's not the same Jesus of Nazareth."

Brock leans in trying not to miss a word.

"Resisters"—the professor raises his voice—"are an enemy to humanity. Peter Roma has sent the Christ energy, 'like a thief in the night,' to cleanse the earth of its negative energy brought on by the resisters. By eliminating their physical bodies, he's helping their souls reincarnate into a higher state of consciousness."

Brock's eyebrows pull together, and his forehead crinkles. *"He's helping their souls reincarnate into a higher state of consciousness?"*

"And," the professor continues, "Peter Roma has 'proved' he is Jesus. Don't you remember when he rained fire down from the skies? Or when he walked on water and saved the little girl who drowned?"

Brock reflects on the news footage of a child who'd fallen off a boat and into the Tiber River. The film captured Peter Roma walking out on the water as though it were only two inches deep. He kneeled and reached into the water and pulled up the limp body of a four-year-old girl. He carried her to shore then laid her down on the ground. He kneeled beside her and put his hands on her head and commanded her to wake up. She suddenly coughed up water and cried out.

"Can you 'prove' your sky fairy exists? Why can't you Christian fundamentalists back up your extraordinary claims he exists with some extraordinary proof or even some sort of evidence that can be backed up? Why even our space brothers proved their existence."

Brock glances toward the cell directly across from him. A tall man with pink complexion seems to be engrossed in the conversation. Brock notices folds of his skin hanging on his tattooed arms as if he had been grossly overweight at one time.

The man catches Brock's glance.

Brock nods and smiles.

The man smiles back revealing mustard-colored teeth.

"Professor, I can't prove Jesus to you, but I have faith in what the Bible says and that is that Jesus is coming back to earth in the clouds and every eye shall see Him."

"Why do you fundamentalists continue to cling to the old teachings? It just creates division and negative energy."

The professor's tone changes, and he speaks as though Cornelius were some sort of ignorant student in his class.

"There was a very good reason Peter Roma replaced the Bible with the New Gospel. Throughout history the Bible had been mistranslated and misunderstood and eventually lost its real meaning. The New Gospel reflects the correct and true message originally intended.

"Now, according to the New Gospel, 'cloud' symbolizes confusion, not a literal cloud. Lord Maitreyas appeared at a time of confusion just as the Scriptures said the Christ would.

"And 'Every eye shall see him' has two meanings. Lord Maitreyas fulfilled this scripture literally when every eye saw him on the Day of Pentecost and also symbolically because those who had their 'third eye' open recognized him."

"Professor, the New Gospel is a bunch of lies, a twisted version of Scripture created to deceive people. Peter Roma replaced the Bible because it contradicts his claim that Maitreyas is the Christ. The Bible *clearly* says Jesus is the Christ."

A loud huff comes from the professor's cell. Brock can tell he is annoyed.

The professor clears his throat then says in a loud angry tone, "If you'd read the New Gospel you would know that 'Christ' is not a person but an office; it is an office of the hierarchy of the ascended masters. Lord Maitreyas has held that office for more than two millennia."

His voice changes to its normal tone. "In Peter Roma's last incarnation as Jesus of Nazareth, Lord Maitreyas overshadowed his consciousness and guided his actions during his death and resurrection; that's how people became confused and thought Jesus was the Christ."

Jesse nudges Brock and whispers, "Oh, brother, he sure has an answer for everything, doesn't he?"

Brock nods.

"We're not confused, professor. Jesus warned us not to be deceived, that many would come in His name and claim to be the Christ."

Cornelius raises his voice. "Jesus is returning in the sky the way He ascended, not in an airplane, not in a UFO. Peter Roma is NOT Jesus, and Maitreyas is NOT the Christ. Jesus of Nazareth is the one and only TRUE Christ!"

"The problem with you fundamentalists is that you think if you shout the loudest that equates truth. A lot of nonsensical talk. You are so wedded to your erroneous interpretation of Scripture that you cannot comprehend the return of the Christ now or in the manner in which it has taken place.

"Not only has Lord Maitreyas fulfilled Bible prophecy concerning the return of the Christ, he has fulfilled the Buddha prophecy as the exalted one that would be named Maitreyas and the Muslim prophecy as the Imam Mahdi who would be aided by Jesus. They even scientifically proved that Lord Maitreyas is Osiris, fulfilling the Egyptian prophecy of the god that shall rise again.

"Lord Maitreyas has fulfilled each and every one of these prophecies so until you can 'prove' your sky fairy exists, your claim of a god coming back in the sky is a discombobulated load of made-up nonsense that is not going to get past someone with some semblance of intelligence."

Mario adds, "Yeah. . .what the professor said."

A look of disappointment shows on Cornelius's face. "You'll have your proof someday, professor, but then I'm afraid it will be too late."

Cornelius turns and walks to the back of the cell out of Brock's view. Arturo follows.

"Hey! Where you going?" The bars next door rattle. "Where you going?"

"Mario, I'm done."

"Wait! You can't leave. You're supposed to 'save' me!"

Cornelius reappears.

"Mario, all I can do is share the true Jesus with you. It's up to you to accept Him or reject Him. It appears you have already made up your mind so I'm moving on."

Brock hears the squeaking of the food cart.

"Inmates, keep it down," a guard scolds.

"Yes, sir." Cornelius lowers his voice. "Mario, I will pray for you and the professor." He moves out of view.

"Hey. . .hey!" Mario hollers, ignoring the guard's request to keep it down.

Eventually the food cart makes it way to the front of Brock and Jesse's unit. The guard sports the traditional World Union tanned uniform; his light blue beret covers his blond crew cut.

After straightening his beret, the guard bends over and picks up a tray then slides the yellow plastic through the slot.

Retrieving the tray from the floor, Brock turns and passes it to Jesse. He reaches for the second tray when suddenly a hand slips through the bars and grasps his wrist.

Stunned, Brock looks up into the face of a handsome young man. His dazzling, crystal-blue eyes smile at him. Brock thinks he looks familiar, but he's not sure where he's seen him before.

The guard leans forward. "Four of you will be tried by fire. Three of you will not burn. Of the three, two will fall and one will be spared."

His voice changes to a mournful cry. "But woe to the fourth one who will be scorched by the fiery furnace where there is weeping and gnashing of teeth."

His voice resumes its clear tone. "Follow the iron snake to where the bear flows with gold." The corners of his mouth turn up, and his eyes look like pools of translucent water.

He squeezes Brock's wrist before he returns to the food cart and wheels it forward.

Trembling, Brock calls after him. "Who are you? What does that mean?"

The guard disappears down the hall.

Who was he?

He repeats the guard's words. *"Four of you will be tried by fire. Three of you will not burn."*

What did he mean? *"One will be scorched by the fiery furnace where there is weeping and gnashing of teeth. . .Follow the iron snake to where the bear flows with gold."*

Bewildered, he scoops up the tray from the floor and sits down in the chair next to Jesse. Balancing the tray on his lap, he scans the meal and decides to save his orange for later. Opening the milk container, he pours the white liquid into a cup.

"Jesse, what do you think of when I say, 'follow the iron snake to where the bear flows with gold'?"

"Beats me. . .why?"

"I wish I knew."

Brock picks up the cup and sips.

"GARBAGE! DISGUSTING GARBAGE! GIVE US BACON AND EGGS!" blasts the Hispanic accent from the cell next to theirs.

"Sounds like Mario!" Brock laughs out loud and glances over at Jesse. Jesse's eyes are closed, and his hands are folded in his lap.

Setting his milk down, Brock shuts his eyes.

"Dear merciful Father in heaven," Jesse prays. "We praise Your holy name."

Shame rises from Brock's consciousness as Jesse prays to the one he denied.

"We thank You, Father, for this food You have given us. We humbly accept it. We pray for Mario and the professor and all those in darkness that they may see the light. In Jesus' name, amen."

Opening his eyes, Brock reaches for the white package. Bold, black letters proclaim OATMEAL, with "Distributed by World Union Food Program" printed at the bottom.

Ripping the package open, he pours the contents into the bowl then soaks it with milk. With the plastic utensils he spreads peanut butter and jelly on the two slices of bread then sandwiches them together.

"So how's your headache?" Jesse asks while preparing his oatmeal.

"My headache? Oh, yeah, my headache. That's odd—it's gone."

He remembers the guard; it seemed like his headache disappeared when the guard touched his wrist. *Who was he?* He prods his memory when an image of the bailiff surfaces. *The bailiff? Nah. What would the bailiff be doing here at the prison?*

Taking a bite of his sandwich, Brock reflects on the conversation in the hall.

"I wonder what the professor is in for," he asks Jesse.

"For not predicting the Cubre Veijo Tsunami."

"What?" His brows rise.

"Yeah, crazy, I know."

"Yeah."

He recalls when a mountain the size of Rhode Island collapsed into the Atlantic Ocean. It sent five-hundred-foot tsunami waves into the Eastern Seaboard destroying New York City and the coastline.

"So do you know what the professor meant when he said Maitreyas was the god Osiris? Wasn't Osiris some sort of Egyptian pharaoh or something?" He takes another bite of his sandwich.

"Yes, he was." Jesse sets his spork down next to his bowl then wipes his mouth on his sleeve. "From what I understand, Osiris was the first pharaoh of the Egyptians, and they believed he was part human and part god."

"Why did they think he was part god?"

"They believed gods came down from the sky and took mortal wives and had children with them. Amun Ra, the sun god, was the king of kings of these gods. They believed Osiris was descended from Ra, making Osiris a god. You know the obelisk?"

Brock nods.

"It symbolized a sun ray, and they believed Ra's spirit dwelled in it."

"That's odd. . .there was an obelisk in my dream last night."

"You'll have to tell me about it."

"Yeah, I will," Brock replies thoughtfully.

"What's interesting is that Ra means light and Lucifer means light and the Bible says Lucifer disguises himself as an angel of light [2 Corinthians 11:14]. Oh! I almost forgot— one of Allah's ninety-nine names, An-Nur, also means 'the light.' Now what's even more amazing is that these pharaohs took names that reflected their belief in their divinity."

Jesse pauses.

31

"For instance, Pharaoh Rameses—I'm sure you've heard of him?"

Brock visualizes the famous three-thousand-year-old mummy that's displayed at the Cairo Museum in a glass casing."

"Yeah, sure, I'm familiar with him."

"Rameses means 'son of Ra,' and there was the Pharaoh Akhenaten—his name means 'beautiful are the forms of Ra.' And then there's a name that means 'chosen one of Ra' and so on and so on. You get the picture."

Brock shifts in his chair. "So let me see if I understand this right. The Egyptians believed Ra was some sort of sun god who came to earth and took a human wife? That sounds a lot like the account in Genesis 6."

"Yes, you're right. Many biblical scholars say the Egyptian gods were really the fallen angels of Genesis 6." Jesse picks up his bowl and begins to shovel the oats into his mouth.

Brock tries to recall Genesis 6:1. *The sons of God saw the daughters of men and married them, and they bare giant children with them which were the mighty men of old.*

Brock draws a long gulp of milk then sets the empty cup on the tray and belches. "So why do they think Maitreyas is Osiris?"

"Who's complaining about the food?" A harsh voice startles Brock. He chokes on the food in his throat then swallows.

Standing behind the cell bars, a red-faced guard stares at them, his jaws clenched, clutching a pistol.

"Not us," Jesse responds quickly. "The food is delicious!" Jesse holds the half-eaten sandwich out for the guard to see.

The guard moves on to the next cell.

"Who's complaining about the food?" the guard

demands.

Brock strains his ears to hear. The voices are muffled.

"POP! POP! POP!" Three deafening sounds like fireworks reverberate through the cell. He hears a gasp followed by a dull sound, as that of a heavy object striking the ground.

Brock nearly drops the food tray on the floor.

The guard strides past their cell pushing his pistol back into his holster.

Heart pounding against his chest, Brock hurries to the front of the cell where Jesse joins him.

The acrid smell of gunpowder blankets the air. Cornelius and Arturo stand there, eyes wide open, staring.

"You okay, professor?" Cornelius asks.

"Uh, yes." The professor's voice is brittle. "I—I think so."

"Hey, sorry, dude." Arturo's words sound heartfelt.

"Mario," the professor says sharply. "You just couldn't keep your big mouth shut, could you?"

Arturo and Cornelius lower their heads, turn and walk away.

"The poor lost soul. . . ." Jesse shakes his head.

Still trembling, Brock returns to his chair and sits down. He feels sick to his stomach but forces the rest of his food down. He tries to forget that Mario's dead body lies only a few feet away.

"So why do they think Maitreyas is Osiris?" He repeats his earlier question.

"The story goes that when Osiris died his body was mummified and his spirit went to the underworld where Ra made him king of the underworld. The Egyptians worshipped Osiris as the 'lord of the dead,' and they believed he would return someday. Through the years cults and secret societies who followed this mystery religion have been preparing for his return.

"When Maitreyas was revealed on the Day of Pentecost, many of those cults claimed Maitreyas was the god Osiris returned from the dead. Not everyone was convinced, though. They wanted physical proof."

"So what did they do?"

"Do you remember when they supposedly found the tomb of Osiris?"

Brock recalls a documentary special he'd watched about the discovery of the ancient tomb at the pyramids in Giza.

"Yeah, I vaguely remember. They said they'd found a burial chamber with four pillars, and it was underwater. They thought it was the lost tomb of Osiris. I don't recall ever hearing anything about it after that."

"People started demanding to know what the scientist had found in the tomb and wanted to know why they were keeping it hidden from the public. Finally, under extreme pressure, the scientist and archeologists who had worked on the project revealed they believed they had found Osiris's tomb. But they admitted that when they opened the sarcophagus it was empty; there was no body. They wrote it off as a grave robbery.

"Later on Maitreyas's followers proclaimed Osiris's tomb was empty because he had resurrected from the dead."

"Wow! That reminds me of when they found Jesus' tomb empty." Brock shakes his head. "Amazing.

"Uh, hold on a second." Brock drops a tea bag into a Styrofoam cup then stands and places the tray in his chair. Cup in hand he walks to the sink and fills the cup with water then sets it on the window ledge before returning to his chair.

"So how were they able to 'prove' Maitreyas was Osiris?"

Jesse swallows. "Maitreyas's DNA matched the DNA they supposedly found on the hair and linen left in the sarcophagus."

Brock's eyes widen, and his jaw drops open. "No way! His DNA matched?"

"Yep."

Brock thinks for a second then says, "It wouldn't surprise me if they found Osiris's body, cloned it and had a secret ceremony summoning up the spirit of Osiris from the underworld to possess it."

Jesse nods in agreement. "Anything is possible."

Finishing off the last piece of crust, Brock picks up his bowl of oatmeal and begins stirring the oats. "I was thinking, if Osiris is the prophesied antichrist, why isn't he mentioned in the Bible?"

"He is."

Brock's brows shoot up.

"'Osiris' in the Egyptian tongue is Asar; in the Hebrew tongue it's Asshur. The Bible describes Asshur as the Assyrian king who built many cities in Assyria including Nineveh.

"I can't remember the verses." Jesse frowns. "There's one in Isaiah and one in Micah. They say that in the last days the Assyrians will invade Israel" [Isaiah 10:5-6; Micah 5:5].

Brock stares at the floor. "And the beast that was, and is not, even he is the eighth, and is of the seven, and goeth into perdition" [Revelation 17:11].

"Osiris 'once was' and 'was not' at the time John wrote the prophecy, 'and will come up out of the abyss and go to his destruction.'"

Brock looks at Jesse. "So how come you know so much?"

A glum look crosses Jesse's face, and he looks at the floor. "My old man belonged to one of them secret societies."

"Oh."

"Yeah." He looks up. "I had always thought it was just a good ol' boys' club until after he died when I found some of his books. The books exposed the plans of the New World Order and how they were preparing for the return of Osiris. After an initiate reached a certain degree, maybe thirty-three, the great architect of the universe is finally revealed as Lucifer.

"Guess what one of their secret pass words is?"

"What?"

"Abaddon."

Abaddon. Brock recalls the verse. "And they had a king over them, which is the angel of the bottomless pit, whose name in the Hebrew tongue is Abaddon, but in the Greek tongue hath his name Apollyon" [Revelation 9:11].

"Man, I sure would like to have gotten my hands on one of those books for my paper."

Scraping the bottom of his bowl he shoves another bite of oatmeal into his mouth.

"Brock, I hope you don't mind me asking you this, but if you believe Maitreyas is the antichrist, why did you agree to accept Maitreyas in court?"

The oats stall in Brock's throat. *Jesse was at his court trial.*

A stabbing pain pierces his heart. Avoiding Jesse's gaze, he stares at the floor. His mouth opens to speak, but no words come out.

CHAPTER

4

Sweat soaks Brock's shirt, and his eyes stare straight ahead at the yellow, tea-stained wall as he jogs in place. This was a habit he'd started in solitary confinement; it helped clear his head and pass the boredom of the day.

In his mind he visualizes himself jogging on the bike path that runs along Santa Monica Beach. He erases from his memory the stained red sand and the rotting carcasses of fish, dolphins and whales scattered along the Pacific coastline. Instead he focuses on how it was before God's two prophets turned the sea into blood in retaliation for the persecution of the Christians and Jews by the World Union.

He forms a mental image of kids picking up sea shells and a sandpiper dodging the waves scrounging for sand crabs. He hears a couple on their tandem bike yell "to the left" as they zoom past him. He can almost taste the cool salty air as he runs on the worn asphalt toward the grove of orange trees. He loved running by the trees and pictures the white cluster of flowers that bloomed and gave an intoxicating sweet aroma.

The orange he'd saved from breakfast tweets his memory. Breathing heavily, he stops running in place, walks over and plucks the round fruit from under his pillow then sits down in the chair next to Jesse.

Peelings drop to the floor as his fingers dig into the orange.

He holds out a wedge. "Would you like a piece?"

"No, thanks. I already had mine." Jesse leans back and closes his eyes.

Juice squirts as Brock bites into a slice.

"You sure got one nasty scar there."

"Yeah." Jesse opens his eyes. He fingers the jagged, red line above his brow.

"How'd you get it?"

"I slammed my Harley into a tree."

Brock swallows. "Did someone run you off the road?"

"No." Jesse pauses for a moment then says, "I actually hit the tree on purpose."

"What? You hit a tree on purpose? Were you trying to kill yourself?"

Jesse sits up. "No, I guess you could say I was a little out of control. No, I take that back. I was totally out of control. I, uh, I did it for drugs."

"Drugs? You? So how'd you get into drugs?" Brock jams another orange slice into his mouth.

"Well, you see, I used to go to a lot of Hollywood parties—"

"Were you an actor or something?"

"Yes."

"Really?" He is curious. "What movies did you play in?"

Jesse laughs. "Well, my best role was in *Zen Warrior*."

"*Zen Warrior?* I remember that movie. . .that was you?!"

"Yes, that was me." Jesse smiles. "Back then I was young, but now I'm just an old washed-up actor."

Brock wipes his mouth with the back of his hand. "I knew you looked familiar! So what happened?"

"I was on top of the world making movies and going to parties. At one of those parties someone slipped me a little white box with a black bow on top. I didn't see who it was, but I saw a hang tag on the box. When I read it, I thought it was some kind of joke or something. The tag said, 'To J.C. from the devil.'"

J.C.? Brock searches his memory then recalls the initials of the once popular actor. *Jesse Chapman.*

"So what was in the box?" Brock sticks the last piece of orange into his mouth.

"Inside the box was a large rock of cocaine. That was my first encounter with drugs."

Brock goes back to his first encounter with drugs. He was at a party, and a girl pulled him into the bathroom where a mirror lined with white powder was sitting on the edge of the sink. She nonchalantly handed him a straw and said, "Sniff." He knew Aunt Millie would disapprove; she was always reminding him that his body was the "temple of God." But he wanted to impress this girl and didn't want her to think he was lame so he snorted the cocaine. After that he remembers he felt so guilty for letting Aunt Millie down, especially after she took him and his sister in when his mother died.

Jesse continues. "Soon I couldn't eat, I couldn't sleep, and when I did finally fall asleep I had the most horrible nightmares. I stopped getting good roles in Hollywood. At the time I didn't care—all I cared about was my heroin and cocaine.

"Deep down I was terrified I would die. Eventually I checked myself into one of them drug rehabilitation centers. That worked for only a little while. When the North American Union enacted the death penalty for drug possession, I found it more and more difficult to find them. I was desperate. I knew it would only be a temporary fix, but I figured I could get some legal drugs if I was in the hospital so I crashed my Harley into a tree.

"As I said, it was only a temporary fix. Not a day went by that I didn't crave drugs. One day I'd decided to surrender everything to Jesus if He'd save me from the hell I was in. I cried out and begged Him to save me.

"I didn't see any lightning flashes or hear any ringing bells, but after a few days people began to notice a change in me. I noticed too. I began to walk and talk to Jesus, and little by little He revealed more and more truth to me. I started going to a Bible study group for believers in the entertainment business. It was a miracle. I finally found peace."

Brock jumps up and walks over to the narrow window. "So what're you in for?"

"For blasphemy and resister of the New World Order. I haven't been sentenced yet, but I'm sure it's death by beheading. I came straight here from one of them re-education camps."

Brock picks the Styrofoam cup off the ledge, walks back and sits down. "I'd heard about those re-education camps. So what was that like?" He sips the warm, grassy liquid.

"It reminded me of rehab except the higher power we were to acknowledge and accept was replaced with Lucifer."

"Wow. How blatant is that."

"Yeah. I swore I would never ever bow down to Lucifer or his fake Christ so I got an F"—Jesse fingers the letter F over his chest—"in re-education, and I wear it proudly!" He grins.

Brock smiles and sips his tea.

Jesse's hand moves to his lower back and rubs. "So what was your dream about? You know, the one with the obelisk?"

A serious look crosses Brock's face. He leans forward, and his right hand grasps his cup while his elbows rest on his knees.

Jesse lets out a small groan. "Hold on a second. My back is killing me." Jesse retrieves his pillow from the bed then sits down again and stuffs the pillow behind his back. "That's better. Go on."

"I'll start from the beginning. I was following a trail—it looked like it was in the middle of an old lava flow. I was extremely thirsty, and apparently water was supposed to be at the end of the trail. So I'm walking up this trail, and I hear someone singing. As I hurried I saw it was Lorraine—"

"Lorraine?" Jesse's eyebrows lift.

"Yes, Lorraine. I hurried to catch up with her when I saw a man sitting off to the side of the trail. He looked at me and held up a water bottle." Brock drops his voice an octave or two. "'I am Aquarius, the Water Bearer,' he said, 'and my duty is to guide you to the water of life. Go back down the trail to the great city that's perched on seven hills. There you will find the river of truth, and your thirst will be quenched.'

"I said, 'Thanks, but no thanks,' and kept on.

"I saw Lorraine had stopped singing and was on her knees. That's when I noticed a wall of flames blocking the trail. I kept trying to catch up to her, but it felt like I was on a treadmill. My legs were moving, but I didn't feel as if I was getting anywhere. Then I saw Lorraine stand up and walk right through the flames! I hurried, but by the time I got to the fire Lorraine was completely out of sight. I remember thinking that if Lorraine could walk through the fire so could I. But when I put my hand out I burned myself. That's when I decided to go to the river the man had told me about."

Brock pauses for a minute and lifts the cup to his lips, takes a long sip of tea then sets the empty container on the floor.

"So I turned around and started walking back. I passed where the man was meditating, and he was gone. I kept walking till I came to a fork in the trail; a sign read 'Great City.' I took that trail and found the river. I drank the water, and at first it was very sweet; but then it turned bitter. I was so thirsty I drank it anyway. I drank and drank, but I was still thirsty.

"I remember hearing music like tambourines and flutes coming from the city so I headed there. Above the city gate a sign read, 'Sodom and Egypt.' Two Roman soldiers stood at the entrance, and the people inside were wearing tunics and robes. When I saw the Wailing Wall I realized I was in ancient Jerusalem.

"I saw some boys dancing around an obelisk singing. That's where I saw the obelisk I told you about. I saw another group of people dancing around a giant, bronze statue of a man with a bull's head; he was sitting down with his arms stretched out over a fire pit.

"A woman bowed to the idol then put a small bundle into the arms of a woman who appeared to be a queen. When the queen turned to accept the bundle I saw she had three faces—"

"Three faces?"

"Yeah, three faces. The woman said a prayer. I caught a few words. 'Oh, queen of heaven, bringer of light, I give to you my sacrifice.' Then the woman turned to a man whose back was to me. He was wearing a long-purple robe, and he handed her a piece of paper and marked something on her forehead.

"Then the queen with three faces placed the bundle into the outstretched hands of the statue.
The music stopped, and all eyes were on the statue. Then they started chanting something low—it sounded like they were saying, 'Yah-buh-lun, Yah-buh-lun.'

"All of a sudden the earth began to shake, and I heard a big groaning sound, and the statue came to life. The bull man stood up, and then he dropped the bundle into the fire.

"And then"—Brock paused and looked straight at Jesse—"I heard a blood-curdling scream. That's when I realized he had just dropped a baby into the fire. I was horrified and gasped out loud—that's when everyone turned and stared at me. I could tell they were angry.

"Then the robed man turned around. At first I thought he was Jesus, but then I realized it was Peter Roma. He pointed at me and shouted"—Brock drops his voice an octave and all but shouts—"'Have you made your sacrifice to the Lord?'

"I lied and said yes.

"Then he demanded I prove it and show him a certificate. I didn't have a clue what he was talking about so I bolted out of there; I knew if they caught me they would kill me.

"The next thing I knew I was falling—I landed at the bottom of a big hole. When my eyes adjusted to the dark I saw an entrance to a cave. I remember thinking that maybe it was a way out. I could hear sounds coming from inside like people laughing and screaming and music like violins and fiddles being played. But they were all out of tune—it was one big loud racket.

"I ventured into the cave and followed the tunnel down toward the noise. That's when I turned a corner and saw a man—"

Brock stops and breathes in deeply.

"Don't stop now!" Jesse exclaims.

Brock exhales. "Okay, where was I?"

"You saw a man."

"Yes, I saw a man—he was on fire, but he wasn't burning. And they—these ugly demon-like creatures were terrorizing this man. They were hitting him and biting him and cursing at him. The man was hunched over and obviously in pain. I knew I'd stumbled upon something taboo so I slowly started to back away when the man raised his head—"

Brock's face begins to contort.

"This man, he looked at me and yelled at the top of his lungs, 'Brock! Go back! Don't come here!'"

Brock leaps out of his chair and paces back and forth like a caged lion.

"Who was the man?" Jesse asks.

Brock's voice cracks, and a single tear escapes his eye. "The man. . .the man was my dad. . . ."

"Oh, wow. . .your dad. What happened after that?"

"I woke up."

"What do you think your dream means?"

"Uh, I don't know. . .that my dad is in hell where he belongs?" His voice is bitter. Seeing his father in his dream was like opening an old wound that had never healed and pouring salt in it.

"I sense you don't have a good relationship with your dad?"

"I can't stand the man."

Tension fills the air. Brock stares out the window. Yes, he hated his dad for driving his mother to suicide. If only he'd loved and supported his family more than he did booze and other women.

The bloodied, bruised image of his mother pops into his head. She points a gun at his dad then turns the pistol to her own head and pulls the trigger as he and his sister watch in horror. . . .

After a few minutes Jesse breaks the silence. "I think I know who the guy called Aquarius is."

"Yeah?" Brock walks back over and sits down in the chair and faces Jesse.

"That had to be Maitreyas."

"Maitreyas?"

"Yes. In the old Buddhist prophecies the coming fifth Buddha was called the water bearer. Many statues show the Maitreya Buddha with a water flask."

"What about the bull statue?" Brock's eyes probe Jesse's.

"The bull statue sounds like Baal." A disturbed look crosses Jesse's face. "You said they were chanting Jahbullon? You know that secret society my old man belonged to? Jahbullon is their unholy trinity: Yah stands for Yahwah, Buh for Baal and On was for Osiris.

"And the queen you saw? She was probably Osiris's wife, Isis, also called the queen of heaven."

Bewildered, Brock gets up and walks over to the window and stares outside. "I wonder why I dreamed those things."

Jesse yawns then says, "Don't know." He gets up and walks to the set of beds. Stepping on the lower bunk he pulls himself up to the top bunk and lies down.

Blinking heavily, Brock climbs onto his own bed and stretches out. He turns over on his side.

Closing his eyes, images of his father materialize in his mind. *Is my father in hell?* he wonders. He hasn't seen or heard from him in more than ten years. His conscious quickly submits to sleep. . . .

Jesus answered and said unto her, Whosoever drinketh of this water shall thirst again: But whosoever drinketh of the water that I shall give him shall never thirst; but the water that I shall give him shall be in him a well of water springing up into everlasting life.
John 4:13-14

CHAPTER

5

A thundering sound like a freight train barreling through the walls abruptly wakes Brock from his nap. His heart rate speeds up bringing him fully alert. A deep, heavy muffling noise echoes beneath him. His bed sways with short, quick jerks, and the cell bars jolt rapidly in a succession of sharp clangs.

"EARTHQUAKE!" Jesse yells.

Brock rolls off his bed at the same time Jesse plummets from the top bunk to the floor.

The men bend and spread their legs apart extending their arms out like two surfers riding a big wave.

Up and down, up and down, the floor revolves and vibrates beneath them.

The building heaves a prolonged dull cry as if it's in sheer agony. White dust rains from the ceiling above. A pipe bursts under the sink, spraying water in every direction.

Slowly the trembling ground calms, and the rumbling fades.

Brock stands up straight. "It must be over."

"Yeah." Jesse walks over and picks up his shoes out of the puddle of water. He climbs up to the top bunk and hangs his legs over the side. "Boy, that was a big one! At first I thought I was just dizzy, and then I realized it was an earthquake."

"Ugh." Brock grimaces. "What's that smell?" He steps

to the window and peers outside. The sun casts short shadows on the empty concrete yard. In the distance a guard tower has toppled over on its side crushing the electric security fence.

Suddenly an earsplitting, hollow sound echoes throughout the building. Brock's body lifts off the ground then is violently propelled backward through the air. Shards of glass fly with him like small pellets fired from a shotgun. Slamming against the bars, he slumps to the ground as if he were a rag doll.

An orange ball of fire roars down the corridor. The flames scream and lick the ceiling like demons dancing in an evil, rapturous delight before disappearing.

Brock hears a loud high-pitched scream that sounds like someone in intense pain coming from down the hall, maybe five or six cells down.

A black vapor quickly fills the air and wraps itself around Brock's crumpled body. He feels an agonizing pain in his left shoulder that had carried the brunt force of his weight when he hit the bars.

Forcing his eyes open he expels a huge cough from his lungs.

"Brock!" Jesse hollers. "Brock, are you okay?"

"Yeah." He utters a deep mournful sound. "I think so. I hurt my shoulder."

Water hisses from under the sink.

Pushing his body into an upright position, Brock tries to swallow, but his tongue sticks to his teeth. Ignoring the pain, he moves to his feet and hobbles over to his bunk. He grabs his shoes from under the bed and slips them on.

"Help! Will someone please help. . . ?" a desperate voice cries out followed by coughing.

Brock looks toward the hall. A blanket of black fills the corridor and seeps into the unit.

"HELP! SOMEBODY, HELP!" another voice yells.

Pulse pounding in his veins, Brock yells, "Our cell block is on fire! We've got to get out of here!" His voice shakes with a slight, quavering movement.

Jesse lets out a series of coughs.

Brock studies the window. The glass had blown out, but it would be impossible for them to squeeze their bodies through the five-inch opening.

"We need to block the window! It'll slow down the fire." He tugs on the bottom mattress. "Jesse, tell the others to do the same."

Jesse drops to the floor and yells into the smoky hall. "Cover your windows with the mattresses from your beds!"

"What for?" a voice asks.

"To stop the oxygen from fueling the fire!"

"Oh, uh. . .okay!"

The room darkens.

Brock walks to the front of the cell and yells into the hall, "After you block your windows, soak your blanket with water then wrap yourselves and wait on the floor next to your door!" Like a blind man, Brock feels his way back to the bunks and pulls at the blankets then saturates them at the sink with water from the broken pipe.

Carrying the dripping blankets he steps to the front of the cell.

"Jesse?"

"I'm here."

"Here's your blanket." Brock holds out his arm and waits for Jesse to take it.

After arranging his own blanket over his shoulders Brock lowers himself to his knees then lies down on the floor next to Jesse. The smoke burns his eyes, and the fumes are strangling him. He feels like a rat in the coils of a snake squeezing the breath out of him. He buries his face under the wet blanket.

An inmate bangs on the bars. CLANG! CLANG! CLANG!

CLANG! CLANG! CLANG!

"Let us out! We're gonna burn to death! Let us out!" Others join in.

CLANG! CLANG! CLANG!

Stay calm, Brock tells himself. *Somebody will find us.*

Sweat soaks his clothes. He tries to ignore the cracking and hissing sounds of the fire as it draws closer and closer.

Breathe—take steady breaths and remain calm. He tightens the cloth around his face.

Jesse lets out a cluster of coughs then says, "Dear Lord, please help us. . . ."

Brock is trembling. *What if nobody rescues us? Is God punishing me for denying Him in court?*

A feeling of hopelessness settles in.

His thoughts go back to the trial. *"I don't want to see you die,"* the prosecutor said. *"The judge does not want to see you die, and Lord Maitreyas does not want to see you die. Brock, do you want to die?"*

No, of course not. He didn't want to die. He wasn't supposed to die. He was supposed to flee to the mountains. Getting arrested was not in his plans. His plans were to continue reporting the news and write his newspaper; then when the law requiring all citizens to have Maitreyas's mark went into effect he would hide in the woods and hunker down in his underground shelter. He'd stocked it with plenty of food and water and all kinds of survival gear; he was fully prepared. He even had a bug-out bag, a small pack loaded with essentials for survival, next to the front door, and his motorcycle was all gassed up and ready to go. He was never supposed to get arrested. . . .

The snapping of the fire brings him back to the real world. He notices the constant clanging of the bars has stopped. *Have the inmates died of smoke inhalation?* The idea of burning alive terrifies him. He decides that when the fire gets close enough he'll stand up, breathe in the smoke as hard as he can and then die from the fumes so he won't feel the fire burn his flesh.

"Brock. . .I think I hear someone."

Brock strains his ears. . .muffled voices then banging iron. *Somebody is coming!* His heart leaps in his chest. *We're rescued!*

He lunges to his feet, the blanket slipping off his face. He takes a whiff of the intoxicating smell of rotting flesh mixed with gaseous smoke. Gagging, he pulls the blanket back over his head and covers his nose as he peers down the hall trying to see, but there is zero visibility.

"Over here!" men's voices yell frantically. "Over here!"

Brock and Jesse join in. "Over here! Over here!"

Footsteps in the corridor stop in front of the cell next door.

Iron wheels squeak as a door rolls open. The professor shuffles past.

The heavy footsteps move across the hall to Cornelius and Arturo's cell. Iron wheels squeak. Arturo and Cornelius move quickly past their cell and down the hall.

"Over here!" Brock yells impatiently. "Over here!"

The steps move to Brock and Jesse's cell. With a click the barred door rolls open.

"Inmates, move to the exit," a voice says through the smoke.

The blanket falls to the floor as Brock hurries into the thick smoke. A hand grasps his elbow, and a voice whispers in his ear, "Follow the iron snake to where the bear flows with gold." The strong grip releases his arm.

51

"Wait!" Brock calls into the dark like a blind man. "What do you mean?"

Silence.

"Brock, are you coming?" It's Jesse.

Overcome by the deadly fumes Brock coughs out of control. Battling to catch his breath he yells, "Jesse, where are you?"

"I'm right here!" Jesse replies.

A phrase from a fire drill at the news station taps Brock's memory. *"Crawl down low when it's time to go."*

"Jesse, we need to get down on the floor."

The ground scorches Brock's hands and knees as he lowers himself to the floor.

"I'll lead the way. Grab onto my pant leg so we don't get separated."

He hears a cough then feels a tug on his right pant leg.

Using the wall of bars as a guide Brock crawls on all fours: right hand, right knee, left hand, left knee. He pushes forward through the heavy smoke; his knees grind on the floor. He continues crawling, right hand, right knee, left hand, left knee.

Brock's hand brushes a wood sill. They crawl through the doorway out of their block and follow a solid wall to the right. Brock feels lost and disoriented in the blackness, but he keeps plodding forward. *How much further?* he wonders. *We should be at the showers by now.*

Brock coughs every few minutes. *Where is everybody?* he wonders. *I haven't seen or heard a soul since we left our unit.*

Watery fluid drips from his forehead. The temperature is rising. He's pretty sure this is the right way—it has to be. He hears crackling and hissing noises. Something is wrong. He stops.

The floor rocks back and forth, and small chunks of

debris and fire shower down from the ceiling.

The men cover their heads under their arms.

After a few minutes Brock lifts his head and sees an orange glow framing a door up on the left. *The elevator.* He remembers passing the elevator after he showered; the showers must be close by.

Sparks stream from the gaps in the door at the sides. The elevator door bursts into flames.

"You still with me, Jesse?"

Brock feels two tugs on the hem of his pant leg. He waits for the embers to burn out in the hall before proceeding. His palms and knees hurt. He tries to swallow, but his tongue feels as if it's stuck to the back of his throat; he's so thirsty.

Heat rises as they crawl past the elevator, now consumed by glowing, burning vapors.

Safe on the other side, Brock pushes pieces of drywall and debris aside, creating a path.

Straight ahead he catches a gleam of daylight filtering through an opening. Images form as his vision clears. Tangled bricks and steel clutter the corridor.

"Jesse, I think we're close to the showers."

The two men leap to their feet and run to the light, fear and despair vanishing as hope sets in.

A pungent smell like burnt liver mixed with a musky perfume stings Brock's nostrils. He enters the small burned-out hulk once lined with cupboards stocked with towels and bathing supplies. Smoldering wood and ceiling tiles are splintered, and the normally white walls are covered with a thick layer of black soot.

Light pours through a gaping hole in the ceiling exposing a black boot wedged in the shower door.

Holding his breath, Brock pulls the door open, his heart pounding in his ears.

The shower room is shrouded in black except for an eerie glow illuminating a half dozen rigid, scorched bodies still smoldering on the floor. Brock stares down at the burned corpse of a man whose hair is a clump of char. His face is blistered and swollen; his mouth hangs open in a frozen scream; his tongue is singed black; yellow fluid drips from his fingers and pools on the tiled floor.

"UGH!" Brock trembles with a sudden convulsion. Nausea rises in his stomach, and he vomits on the floor. His stomach roils; his throat burns. Finally he gets control and wipes off his mouth on his shirt.

"Poor guys." Jessie's lips tighten. "They probably went to the showers hoping the water would save them from the fire."

"Yeah."

Brock walks back into the hallway, with Jesse behind him.

The smoke is thinning, but it's still difficult to see. Walking on the left of the hall, Brock runs his fingers along the wall until he feels a door jamb.

He presses his fingers on the surface then pushes his palms down. He knows that if heat comes from the door the fire is in the room and to move on.

The metal feels warm. He reaches for the knob and turns it till the door creaks open.

Plaster dust covers the desks and filing cabinets with a ghostly pallor. Cupboards hang open revealing empty shelves; supplies are scattered over the floor. A mounted light fixture has snapped loose from the ceiling and hangs by threadlike wires. Riot helmets dangle on hooks on a wall, and on another wall the words "WARNING—NO WARNING SHOTS" are stenciled in bold black letters.

Moaning sounds come from the center of the room. A guard lies on his back on the floor; blood gurgles from his mouth and oozes from a hole in his chest. Brock recognizes him as the one who shot Mario.

The man opens his eyes, looks at Brock then shuts them again.

A squeaking chair captures Brock's attention then a pair of black shoes under a metal desk. Brock hurries over and peers beneath the desk into the face of a man covered with soot.

"Please don't kill me," the guard pleads. "I have a wife and kids."

"Don't worry, mister. We're just trying to escape the fire."

"Look!" Jesse points across the room. "There's the door!"

Brock's eyes follow Jesse's finger.

Forgetting the man under the desk he hurries toward the door. Out of the corner of his eye he spots a five-gallon water bottle lying on the carpet, clear liquid spilling over the floor. His parched mouth reminds him of his thirst.

"Hang on." Brock dashes over and grabs the bottle.

Jesse flings the door open, and the two men rush outside into the blessed air.

CHAPTER
6

An ear-piercing alarm screeches over the dead and wounded men scattered across the concrete yard like toy soldiers.

A prisoner hangs motionless at the top of the electric fence, tangled in the barbed wire. A few gunshots sound in the distance.

It is a hot day, and heat still radiates from the sidewalk. Brock presses the plastic jug to his mouth and gulps the water then passes the container to Jesse.

He glances up at the five-story façade. Smoke billows from its slit window eyes glaring demon-like at the chaos and rubble.

The slap of rubber shoes catches Brock's attention as an inmate speeds past them.

Two more inmates race up the sidewalk: Cornelius and Arturo.

"Hey! Hey, Jesse!" the middle-aged African American calls as he jogs toward them. "You guys made it!"

"Yeah," Jesse replies. "For a while there I thought we were goners."

"Here." Jesse passes Cornelius the jug of water.

Cornelius gulps the liquid down like it's a can of soda pop then passes it to Arturo.

The men instinctively duck as a barrage of gunshots fire in the distance.

"Be careful." Cornelius straightens, his face shiny with sweat. "A few rogue inmates have taken over and are hunting down the guards and killing them, and I hear the guards are shooting at anything that moves."

Brock recalls the guard shot in the chest and the one hiding under the desk. "Good to know."

"So what're you guys planning?" Cornelius looks at Jesse then Brock.

"Uh. . .I don't know." Jesse turns and looks at Brock.

Plan? He hadn't thought about any plans. He was just trying to get out of the building alive. Brock looks past the dead guard lying face down about six feet away. He'd expected armed guards waiting for the inmates outside, telling them where to go; he never thought they'd walk into total chaos. Now the prison was in lockdown.

A picture forms in his head: He and all the prisoners are being rounded up and told to stand against the fence, and then they are all shot dead. That's what they do—no trial, no jury—if you're out of line they'll kill you.

Pulling his shoulders back Brock deepens his voice. "Well, I don't know about you guys, but I'm getting the heck out of this cesspool."

"Yeah, me too," Cornelius replies.

"What?" Arturo balks. "They'll shoot us as rioters if we try to escape."

Cornelius looks down at the lanky Italian. "Look, Arturo. If we stay here we'll either get shot or get our heads chopped off—either way, we die. Do you have any better ideas?"

Jesse nods his head. "Cornelius is right. We don't have much choice."

Brock eyes the tall chain-link fence. His mind goes to the image of the knocked-over watchtower he'd seen from their cell window. He starts up the sidewalk. "I think I know a way out of here."

Cornelius and Jesse follow Brock. Cornelius hollers over his shoulder, "Are you coming, Arturo?"

"Yeah," Arturo grumbles. "I guess so." He tosses the empty water bottle aside.

****

The four men trudge across the prison yard past three gray concrete block buildings with narrow, slit windows. They follow the chain-link fencing that encircles the facility. Brock and Jesse lead the way while Cornelius and Arturo hold back a few paces.

Brock glances back at the demon-like building spewing smoke and flames. They were very lucky to get out of there alive. If it hadn't been for that guard who unlocked their cell they would have been roasted like pigs in the belly of the beast.

The men stop when the fence meets a single-story, gray compound blocking their path.

Brock had figured that if they followed the fence they would eventually come to the watchtower; now he's not so sure what to do. A sign on the fence states, "DANGER—PELIGRO. . . HIGH VOLTAGE KEEP OUT—MORTAL ALTA VOLTAJE NO ENTRE."

Cornelius faces the wire mesh. His brown eyes scan the height.

"Don't even think it, dude." Arturo walks away, shaking his head.

Cornelius replies, "Arturo, the juice is off."

Arturo turns back. "How do you know?"

Cornelius stretches his palms toward the fence.

Arturo's eyes widen.

Cornelius grabs the metal wire with his fingers.

"See! I told you—the juice is off!"

Arturo lets out a puff of air. "I don't care. I still ain't climbing that thing. . .I'm not gonna be no sitting duck."

"Let's go!" Brock interrupts the men and leads them around the perimeter of the gray building. A large A is stenciled in black on the wall next to a door.

Brock pushes against the door, but it won't budge. Cornelius joins him. They slam their bodies against the metal. "It's no use."

The men continue around the building until they reach a block wall topped with barbed wire.

"Over there!" Cornelius points toward a section that has crumbled to the ground.

The men race to the wall. Brock goes first. He scrapes his arm on the twisted rebar as he squeezes through the opening.

On the other side is a fenced-in basketball court. Arturo eases his body into the open gap then Jesse. After a few minutes and a couple of grunts, Cornelius's shaved head pokes through.

The four men hurry across the court to a steel gate. Brock swings it open.

They reach a security cage where spools of razor wire circle the top and security cameras point down on the sidewalk. They enter an enormous dusty field where rows and rows of wire cages about six-feet by six-feet stand.

Brock has heard about this place. It's where they separate prisoners from the general population because they're considered dangerous to the other inmates.

As they walk between the metal enclosures, a low agonizing groan comes from one of the cages.

A horrid smell of urine and feces blasts Brock's nostrils.

The groans get louder and louder sending chills up

and down Brock's spine.

He sees movement.

The men stop and peer into the cage.

A naked man rolls back and forth, his skin covered with massive red lumps. Black flies cluster on open sores on his arms and neck.

The man doesn't acknowledge the four sets of eyes staring down at him; he seems to be out of his mind in agony.

"What's wrong with him?" Brock wonders aloud. "Why isn't he in a hospital or something? Maybe he has a contagious disease and they're isolating him?" He steps back from the cage.

"Poor guy." Jesse shakes his head and steps away too. "I wonder what happened to him."

"I'll bet he has the plague or something," Arturo says.

"He has the mark of the beast."

"What?" Arturo looks at Cornelius.

"Yeah, those sores—they're from taking the mark. That's what'll happen to you, Arturo, if you take the mark."

"Dude, there's no way I'll be taking the mark."

Brock recalls an image of Arturo at Lorraine's execution agreeing to take the mark.

"Arturo, for your sake, I hope and pray you don't. After you take the mark it's too late."

"Like I said, I'll NEVER take the mark."

The men proceed through the maze of pens. In the distance the twisted watchtower lies on its side crushing the security fence. The men break into a run.

Brock arrives first and walks under the metal structure.

"Do you think anyone's in there?" Arturo comes up behind him.

"Nah, they replaced the tower guards with video

cameras and electric fences a long time ago."

"So what if they turn the electricity back on?"

"Then you'll get zapped with five thousand volts of juice." Cornelius grabs Arturo's shoulders from behind.

Arturo jumps then relaxes. "Dude, that's not funny."

"Cornelius," Brock says, "if you lift me up I'm sure I can get to the door."

"Sure thing."

Cornelius steps under the leaning tower.

"If the electricity is off, then how come the alarms are still blaring?" Arturo asks.

"Probably from a battery-powered generator," Jesse says.

"Oh." Arturo still looks confused.

Cornelius bridges himself between the ground and underneath the leaning tower. Brock places one foot in Cornelius's cupped hands then crawls up the giant's back to his shoulders. He reaches up and grabs the metal sides. Balancing himself, he tugs till the door lifts open. With a small grunt he hoists himself inside the round hollow structure. Although he knows Cornelius was kidding, Brock is uneasy coming into contact with the metal surface. *"You'll get zapped with five thousand volts of juice"* plays in his head.

Leaning forward, Brock climbs rapidly through the tower toward the top. He enters an opening and finds himself in a small room with large, tinted windows that are shattered.

With his right foot he kicks the side of one of the windows. After a few kicks the window frame smashes to the ground.

Turning, he descends back to the doorway. *Hurry!* he tells himself over and over again. *"You'll get zapped with five thousand volts of juice."*

"All clear!" he shouts to the men below.

Cornelius lifts Arturo to his shoulders.

Brock grips Arturo's arms and pulls him into the tower.

Arturo begins climbing up.

"I made it!" Arturo calls out from the other side of the fence.

Jesse follows.

Then Brock turns to help his giant comrade, but Cornelius says, "You go ahead. I'll catch up."

The tower staggers as Cornelius pulls himself through the door and into the structure.

Moving quickly, Brock ascends back through the tower and finds his way to the guard room. Careful not to touch the broken glass, he squats then jumps through the window frame to the ground below.

His shoes hit the broken glass with a crunch.

Jesse and Arturo stand in their underwear.

"Dude! Lose your clothes. You're an easy target."

"Yeah, good thinking." Brock pulls his orange prison-issued shirt over his head and steps out of his pants.

Cornelius's legs drop through the window, and he jumps to the ground. He looks at the men in their underwear and without a word rips off his clothes.

The men race north through the field till they reach another fence that surrounds the perimeter of the 350-acre prison site. Brock is astounded they have made it this far. They run hunched over as they follow the fence to the gate.

Tires screech on the asphalt.

"GET DOWN!" Brock commands.

The four men drop flat on their bellies; their eyes are focused on the black asphalt leading out of the prison.

A white SUV loaded with inmates careens down the road leaving sprays of gray in its wake. The vehicle barrels through the open gate past the guard shack. The wheels squeal as it turns onto the highway.

The men look at each other then jump to their feet and bolt toward the gate.

An eerie feeling of getting shot in the back empowers Brock's legs. He gulps for air and runs for his life, dashing past the security building and out onto the open highway to freedom.

CHAPTER

7

Reining in his fear, Brock puts one foot in front of the other as the four fugitives make their way through sparse brush and granite boulders, avoiding the low-hanging branches of the mighty oaks. Occasionally the rumbling noise of a vehicle passes on the highway above them.

The blare of the sirens fades as the men charge down the canyon away from the prison.

Arturo huffs and puffs. Black soot covers his face. "Where're we going?"

"We need to put as much distance between us and the prison," says Cornelius, "because soon this place will be crawling with cops."

The edge of the sun's disk has disappeared below the horizon reminding Brock that it'll be dark shortly; they need to find a place to hide for the night.

A steel drainpipe embedded under the road catches his eye. When he was a kid he and his friends used to play in a similar-looking pipe that ran under a road at a park near his home. It was *their* secret fort. A hand-scrawled sign that read "No Girls Allowed!" was taped to the outside, boldly marking their territory.

"Hold on a second." Brock turns and climbs the steep embankment up to the five-foot wide drain.

A blast of cool air hits his face when he peers into the dark tunnel. Daylight shows at the other end. *An escape route.*

Picking up a small stone he tosses it to scare away any critters that might be lurking in the shadows.

He hears a ping when the stone ricochets off the metal.

"Hello," he calls. "Hello" echoes through the pipe.

He yells down the hill. "This looks like a good place to hunker down for the night."

****

The men sit with their bodies squeezed tight in the drainpipe. Jesse is next to Brock then Arturo; Cornelius is near the entrance.

Seated on the furrowed metal Brock pulls his knees to his chest. When he was a kid the pipe seemed big, and his skinny legs easily stretched to the other side. Now as an adult he is cramped.

He reflects on his childhood fort. He and his friends brought all kinds of stuff from their houses, including two ripped bean bag chairs. They'd sit and play hand-held video games and read their comic books by flashlight while munching on stale potato chips or other food they'd managed to sneak from the kitchen.

"Dude," Arturo says, "did you see that guy in the cage? He must have had some terrible plague or something."

"Arturo," Cornelius replies, "I told you the guy had taken the mark of the beast. The sores are from the chip implant."

"Really? How do you know?"

Arturo and Cornelius remind Brock of a father and a son, Arturo always asking questions and Cornelius always explaining. He wonders how Cornelius has so much patience.

"Because I did research on them and saw them in the

hospital. He is probably one of the volunteers they experimented on under the X-Mark Project."

"The X-Mark Project. . .what's that?"

"It was a top secret program that experimented with DNA tracking effects of the chip implant. They experimented until they perfected it."

"So the chip causes sores?"

"Yes, and I'm sure the World Union is trying to keep it covered up until everyone has received the implant."

The pipe begins to groan and shake violently. At first Brock thinks a heavy truck is passing overhead, but the shaking continues.

"Earthquake! It's another earthquake!" Arturo yells wildly.

Brock's body stiffens as he braces himself against the metal. He imagines the ground ripping open and burying them alive under the road. Then he realizes the pipe is probably one of the safest places to be during an earthquake because of the strong metal sides.

The vibrating metal simmers down.

"It's over." Jesse exhales in a long breath. "It was just an aftershock."

Wrestling with rattled nerves, Brock takes a breath of air and tries to get his mind off the tremor and think about what Cornelius said before they were interrupted.

"Hey, Cornelius, are you a doctor or something?"

"Yes, I was."

"That's impressive. I hope I don't offend you, but I thought for sure you were a football or basketball player, you know with your size and all."

Cornelius laughs. "No, I'm not offended. I get that all the time. My mother wanted me to play football, but my heart was in medicine. I wanted to help people. Besides, I was very clumsy in sports—I had two left feet."

"Wow. Your parents must have been loaded to put you through medical school," Arturo says.

"Actually my parents were very poor. My education was funded by the crown prince of Saudi Arabia."

Brock's ears perk up.

"The prince of Saudi Arabia?" Arturo's voice is filled with awe. "Dude, are you royalty or something?"

"No, no, nothing like that. Saudi Arabia provided twenty million dollars in aid to ten thousand minority students for ten years. When the program came available, my teacher, Miss Jones, helped me apply."

Cornelius pauses then says, "Yeah, good old Miss Jones. . . ."

"Wow, Saudi Arabia—did you ever go there?" Jesse asks.

"Yes, that's where I went to school. I studied at King Saud University in Riyadh."

"Did you have to do anything in return?" Jesse asks.

"Yep, I had to give them ten years of my life. I had to go where they sent me. After my ten years of service I was free to practice wherever I wanted."

After a few minutes Jesse asks, "So how did you end up in the pen?"

"What's ironic is it had something to do with the mark of the beast. You see, one day this guy came into the hospital, and when the nurses changed him into a gown we noticed these boil-like sores all over his body, just like the man in the cage. They started at the soles of his feet and continued to the top of his head.

"He appeared to be in a lot of pain so I put him on sedatives. I took a culture and sent it to a lab. We began right away puncturing the boils to release the fluid and started him on several antibiotics. His vital signs were dangerously low so we put him in ICU. After about a week Patient L wasn't improving so we decided to run him through X-ray—"

"Patient L?" Jesse repeats.

"Yes, he had no name so the staff started calling him Leper Man. We couldn't put that on his chart so we called him Patient L.

"Anyway, we ran him through X-ray, and that's when we discovered an invisible ink tattoo over an implant in the patient's right hand. One of the nurses said he had the mark of the beast. I shrugged it off as a silly superstition. I sent Patient L to surgery to remove the implant. It wasn't easy. I had to call in a plastic surgeon to cut away the scar tissue. When I returned to surgery to remove it, it was gone. What was strange was when I ordered Patient L back into X-ray I discovered the chip had migrated up the patient's arm. It was like it had a mind of its own. I had to use a high-tech sensor X-ray and two monitors to guide me until I finally plucked it out.

"A few days later when I was back on my shift I went in to check on Patient L and discovered he was gone. I thought maybe a family member had claimed him, but I was informed the World Union had taken him into their custody.

"At the time I thought it was odd, but eventually I'd forgotten all about him until another patient came in with sores all over his body and a tattoo and chip implant in his right hand just like Patient L had. The same nurse said it was the mark of the beast. I questioned her about it, and she loaned me her Bible; this was before they were outlawed. She bookmarked Revelation and told me to go home and read it.

"I read Revelation from the beginning to the end. I read about the beast that would come and that a second beast called the false prophet would make everyone have a mark in their right hand or forehead and make them worship the first beast. I read that nobody could buy or sell unless they had the beast's name or number or the mark of his name and that those who received the mark would receive painful sores.

"I began researching the chip implants and reading blogs and watching videos when I realized the first beast of Revelation 13 was Maitreyas and the second beast was Peter Roma. I couldn't believe this was prophesied more than two thousand years ago. It was mind blowing. How could any scientific study explain it? That's when I knew the Jesus of the Bible was the true Christ, and I accepted Him as my Lord and Savior."

"Amen," Jesse says softly.

"So to make a long story short, when the chip implant law passed the hospital staff was mandated to take them. I kept calling in sick until one day the World Union police showed up at my front door. . .the rest is history."

Brock's thoughts return to the man in the cage. It made a lot of sense that the World Union sent him to the prison to keep him out of public view and cover up the side effects from the chip implants. Then again he's surprised they just didn't kill him.

"Dude, that's freaky. How does the chip move all by itself?"

"It gets its energy from the body's temperature. And guess where the two most efficient locations for the temperature exchange are?"

"The hand and the forehead?" Arturo suggests.

"That's right, and they are the two places that clothing does not interfere with heat transferring out of the body."

"So how do they implant the chip?"

"The chip is about the size of a grain of rice. It takes only a few minutes to inject it with a hypodermic needle. They say it is painless. After they implant the chip, a tiny invisible encoded mark is tattooed at the location of the implant. This tattoo monitors your health and also has a global positioning device to track individuals.

"And speaking of tracking devices," Cornelius adds with a yawn, "we need to get rid of these bracelets as soon as possible."

Brock fingers the two rivets that hold his electronic monitoring device on his left wrist. He'd forgotten about the bracelets.

"Will they be able to track us here?" Jesse's voice reveals his concern.

"I think we should be safe here for now; the metal from the drainpipe and the road above should obstruct any GPS signal. Besides, they'll have their hands full until they get the prison back under control."

"I hope you're right."

"By the way," Brock asks, "what's the deal with the different colored bracelets?"

"The colors on the bracelets let the staff know which prisoners need special handling. If you notice, our bracelets are green. That means we need 'special handling' and we are 'dangerous to society.'"

"Ha ha!" Arturo bursts out laughing.

"Hush—keep it down," Cornelius scolds.

"Oh. . .sorry."

Cornelius continues, "The white bracelet, I believe, is for the general population, and the yellow is for inmates with a medical condition. Not sure what the red and blue are for."

Brock thinks about the man in the cage; he remembers seeing a yellow bracelet on his wrist. *Yeah, he had a medical condition all right.*

****

A squeeze on Brock's arm jostles him awake. He feels Jesse beside him.

An engine motor is idling on the highway above them.

His heart races. He hears a deep voice.

"Yep, I checked. This is the location, sir.

"Yes, sir, we'll secure the area."

Fear rushes through Brock. *What if they discover us hiding in the pipe? It will be certain death for all of us.*

He labors to breathe, to stop the trembling inside; it feels like beetles are crawling under his skin.

Movement at the entrance.

"Dude, what're you doing?" Arturo whispers.

"I'll be right back," Cornelius answers. "I'm gonna see if I can distract them."

"No, dude," Arturo pleads. "If they catch you they'll kill you—"

Brock wants to yell at Cornelius to stay in the pipe, but he's gone.

The three men wait, the fear palpable.

Jesse whispers, "Lord, please make us invisible to our enemies, and please shield and protect Cornelius—"

Men's voices shout loudly overhead.

BRATATAT. . .BRATATAT. Machine gun shots reverberate on the walls of the drain pipe.

A loud gasp escapes Arturo.

The three men sit motionless not daring to move.

An excited voice sounds from above. "Yes, sir, we got him. Yes, sir. A black male, sir. No, sir. Yes, sir. We'll need a unit to recover the body, sir. . . ."

Brock's chest tightens. His throat constricts blocking his airway; he can barely breathe.

What just happened? *Cornelius is dead?* But he was just there a few minutes ago.

Keep it together, man. . .keep it together.

Arturo utters a long, low inarticulate murmur.

"Fight it," Jesse whispers. "We've got to keep cool till

they're gone."

Great sorrow fills Brock. He pictures Cornelius lying up there on the road dead. . .he hopes he didn't feel any pain.

He remembers the first time he saw him—at Lorraine's execution.

The men sit frozen for what seems like hours. They fight their urge to weep until finally the idling vehicle pulls away followed by another vehicle behind it.

"They're gone." Jesse's voice is low and solemn.

A deep wail erupts from Arturo. He bawls like a baby and speaks words of unintelligible gibberish. Jesse tries to console him.

It's gut-wrenching listening to Arturo sob. Brock feels his pain. He fights hard to hold back his own feelings of anguish and despair that he's held since his court trial: Lorraine's execution, the earthquake, the fire and now Cornelius's death. He can't take anymore and bursts into tears.

The three men grieve the loss of their friend.

Arturo's voice quivers. "Why did God let Cornelius die? It isn't fair."

"I know," Jesse says. "But we are to trust in the Lord and not rely on our own understanding [Proverbs 3:5]. At least we know he is in a better place now."

Arturo sniffs. "He was such a good man. . .he didn't deserve to die."

"Cornelius was a good man." Jesse pauses then adds, "He sacrificed his life so we can live."

Brock reflects on Jesse's words. *He sacrificed his life so we can live. . . .*

Greater love hath no man than this, that a man lay down
his life for his friends.
John 15:13

CHAPTER

8

Eeeeeeee-ooooo,   EEEEEEEE-OOOOO,
EEEEEEEE-OOOOO. . . .

The deep sound of a siren on the road above startles Brock awake. Dazed at first he begins to see the circular beam of light radiating from the drainpipe's entrance. The pitch of the siren changes as it passes overhead and travels toward the prison.

Brock's fingers wiggle to relieve the numbing, tingling sensation. A sharp pain jabs him as he recollects the events of the night before. *Cornelius is dead.*

A low fluttering noise comes from Jesse.

"Jesse, wake up." Brock gently nudges him.

"Huh?" Jesse rubs his eyes then sits up. His foot taps Arturo's leg. "Arturo, wake up."

Brock's voice is urgent. "We need to get rid of these bracelets as soon as possible. When we leave here the signal should start transmitting our location."

Arturo rubs the sleep from his eyes. "How're we gonna get them off?"

Brock shakes his head. "I don't know. . .we'll just have to figure out a way. If we keep heading down the canyon we should come upon a town, and maybe there we can find something sharp to cut them with."

The three men scramble out of the pipe and into the morning sun and race down the canyon. They stop briefly to drink water from a creek and eat a few ripe blackberries, but the band on Brock's wrist constantly reminds him they are probably being tracked and must keep moving.

In the distance a barbed wire fence catches Brock's attention. *We must be getting close to a town.*

They follow the spiked wire to a small ranch where a black pickup truck is parked next to a doublewide mobile home. A large pile of split wood and a camper held up by four hydraulic jacks are a short way from the mobile home.

"You guys wait here. I'll see if I can find something to cut the bracelets."

Jesse steps down on the bottom wire and pulls up the top wire.

Stooping over, Brock steps through the fence to the other side when he hears explosive barking.

A dog! Am I going to get attacked by a ferocious dog protecting his territory? Jesse and Arturo are depending on me; I can't let them down. We have to get rid of the bracelets.

Picking up a stick, Brock keeps his body low and runs past the wood pile to the camper.

Standing beside the fiberglass exterior, he catches his breath, his heart thumping wildly in his chest. Slowly he peeks around the corner toward the mobile home; a black dog is tied to a rope, barking fiercely.

He's tied up. A deep sigh passes his lips, and he lets the stick fall to the ground.

Hurry, hurry! he yells in his head as his heart accelerates.

Quickly he steps to the door and pulls the metal handle. He hears a clicking sound.

Safe inside, he pulls the door closed behind him. The structure wobbles as he moves into the narrow passage. He scans the inside of the camper: a kitchen with cupboards, a sink and a dining table, and a bed that fits over the cab of a truck. He pulls the knob on a drawer next to the two-burner stove. A flashlight rolls back in the drawer. His hand digs around as he searches for something sharp. His fingers brush aside a travel book and a plastic bottle of mosquito repellent.

The second drawer reveals a can opener and silverware. He pushes the cutlery aside when he sees a sharp-edged, steel blade with a handle. His heart jumps. He grabs the knife and barrels out of the camper and runs as fast as he can toward the fence where Jesse stands with the barbed wire pulled apart.

The men hurry toward a group of trees out of view from the mobile home.

"Jesse, hold out your wrist." Brock breathes heavily.

Jesse extends his arm.

Brock pushes the knife between Jesse's skin and the green bracelet and saws furiously. The sharp blade rips through the plastic covering and begins to shred the braided stainless steel wire.

"Hang on, almost done."

Arturo watches patiently.

With a jerk and snap the bracelet falls to the ground.

Arturo sticks out his left wrist, and Brock begins sawing his bracelet. After a few minutes it falls to the ground.

Quickly Brock hands the knife over to Jesse.

He watches Jesse place the sharp blade on the tracker band.

Arturo picks up the twisted metal off the ground and laughs. "I know—let's duct tape the trackers to the dog's legs and let him loose, and then when the cops come they'll chase the dog all over the place!"

Brock smiles when he pictures the dog running through the woods with their trackers taped to his legs eluding the authorities.

"What makes you think you could get anywhere near that dog? And where you gonna get the duct tape?"

"Oh, I didn't think of that." He sounds disappointed then says, "I know! Let's throw the trackers into the back of a pickup truck!"

"Great idea, but it's just too risky. Besides, what are the odds of a pickup truck coming up the highway? We need to put distance between us and these bracelets."

The back of the knife rubs hard against Brock's skin just before the bracelet snaps and falls to the ground.

He picks up the green plastic and, raising his arm, he pulls it back and pitches the electronic device up the canyon toward the pine trees. With the bracelet gone, it feels like a huge burden has been lifted off his chest. He turns to Jesse and Arturo. "Guys, throw yours in a different direction so it will look like we split up."

Jesse hoists his bracelet forward, and Arturo throws his straight up until it catches on a tree branch.

Arturo laughs. "They'll think I'm hiding in a tree!"

Brock turns. "Let's get the heck out of here."

CHAPTER

9

"Wow! This place looks like it's been nuked." Arturo shakes his head.

"Yeah." Brock wipes his soot-streaked face with the back of his hand.

The three men stand on a street corner at the edge of town under plumes of thick, black smoke. Power poles lie on their sides as though they were whipped back and forth by hurricane force winds; their snake-like lines slither to the ground. Houses are completely deteriorated and lie crumpled on the ground while other homes have slid off their foundations. Shards of glass litter yards from blown-out windows, and people are walking around dazed and confused.

The three men start down the middle of the cracked, buckled asphalt staring in disbelief. On the sidewalks dead bodies are covered with blankets.

A young girl moans and cries in front of a home while men hastily dig through the rubble apparently looking for survivors.

As the men walk from street to street the scene is the same. Whole neighborhoods are in ruins from the earthquake.

A woman stops and stares at them with a strange look on her face.

Arturo stares back. "What's her problem?"

"She's probably never seen three men walking down the middle of the street in their boxer shorts!" says Jesse.

"Yeah!" Arturo laughs then looks at Brock. "Dude, where we gonna find some clothes?"

"I don't know. . .keep your eyes open."

"In the movies, the escaped convicts always found clothes on a clothesline," Jesse adds.

They pass a large smoldering building almost completely burned to the ground. A small sign reads "Deer Creek Apartments." People walk about aimlessly staring and gawking at the black shell.

Suddenly the ground sways beneath Brock's feet; the men instinctively hit the asphalt and ride the seismic waves up and down.

People scream and shout as the earth shudders and groans, jostling everything built upon it. Soon the ground calms, and the men stand and continue walking down the road. The aftershocks started off strong and frequent, but they've tapered down since yesterday's quake. Still the tremors jab Brock's nerves.

"Hey, you, over there!" shouts a raspy, female voice.

Brock turns his head to see a woman standing in her yard staring, clutching a broom.

She hobbles up the cracked sidewalk to the three-foot chain link fence that encloses her property. Her gray hair matches the peeling paint of the single story house.

"Come here a second."

Puzzled, the men walk over to the old woman.

"Oh, dear me," she says, shaking her head. "Are you men from the fire?"

"Uh. . . ." Brock realizes she's probably noticed they are covered in black soot.

"Yes, ma'am, we were in a fire."

"Oh, my, my. Let me get you poor boys some clothes."

The woman turns toward the house with blown-out windows. "Ol' Frank, bless his soul, when he passed he left some clothes that might fit one of you boys. If you'll just follow me around back to the shed."

Brock's eyes widen, and a smile spreads across his face. He looks at Jesse then back to the old woman. "Well, thank you, ma'am."

"Oh, it's nothing. They ain't doing me no good. Besides, just like the good Lord says, 'Sharing is caring!'"

The woman steps over a neatly swept pile of glass and makes her way up the concrete along the side of the house.

"After Frank died I just didn't know what to do with them, and it just didn't seem right to throw them away, you know. . . ."

The men move behind her single file. Arturo whispers out of the woman's earshot, "I think she's one of us."

"No." Jesse points to the two-foot tall statue of a figure adorned with rich ornaments and holding a lotus stalk, knocked over in the side yard. "I think she was referring to Maitreyas as Lord."

"Oh."

The woman stops and ducks under a line of clothes draped from the edge of the house to a rusted white, metal shed.

"Help yourselves, boys. I'd sure like to see someone get some use out of them instead of them just rotting in there."

"Wow! Thanks, ma'am!" Jesse beams.

Brock swings open the shed door.

The old woman turns and starts back up the walk. "Well, ol' Frank, God rest his soul, he went to bed one night and just didn't wake up in the morning. It was that nasty flu, you know. That's how it worked. . .you'd feel sick and. . . ."
The old woman's voice trails behind her as she walks away.

Brock recalls the horrific pandemic that killed millions of people including his little sister Sarah. He was on location in Los Angeles reporting a news story at the Cedar Sinai Hospital. They were turning people away because the facility was full. Rows of sick and dying filled the sidewalks and parking lot. That's when he received a call from the studio informing him Aunt Millie had called; his younger sister Sarah had caught the flu and didn't have much time. He remembers driving like a maniac to San Diego, but by the time he got there it was too late.

Inside the eight-by-ten-foot shed Brock views the items that are covered with a thick layer of dust. A fishing pole leans against the corner next to a rusty, motorcycle frame. Rectangular containers are arranged along the wall with their contents labeled in black ink. Brock's eyes go to the cardboard box marked "Frank" stacked on an antique sewing machine. He moves the box labelled "Christmas decorations" and sets it next to the gas container then pulls down some boxes and stacks them in the middle of the floor. The men each grab a box and start sorting through Frank's belongings.

"Hey, dude, you lied to the old lady about the fire." Arturo rips at one of the cardboard containers and starts pulling clothes out.

"No, I didn't. She didn't say what fire."

Peeling back the lid, Brock removes a faded, denim jacket. Mice droppings fall out, and the material reeks of urine. *Ugh.* His nose wrinkles. Pushing that box aside, he pops open the lid of a plastic barrel sitting next to the sewing machine. There he finds some neatly folded T-shirts. He sets a white one aside and tosses a black one to Arturo.

"Hey, thanks, dude!" Arturo studies the black cotton. "Can I borrow your knife a second?"

"Sure." Brock unwraps the knife concealed in the hem

of his T-shirt and passes it to Arturo then goes back to digging in the barrel until he finds a pair of khaki shorts. An aqua blue material catches his eye with a logo "Beverly Hills Club." He smiles and slips the collared polo shirt over his head.

With a green duffle bag filled with clothes and draped over his shoulder Brock stands. "Are you ladies finished shopping?"

Jesse sports a dark green T-shirt and a baggy pair of blue jeans. "I'm ready."

Brock's glances at Arturo who wears a white ball cap turned backward, baggy black shorts and a gray T-shirt with the arms cut off.

"Yeah, let's go!"

CHAPTER

10

And he shall speak great words against the most High, and shall wear out the saints of the most High, and think to change times and laws: and they shall be given into his hand until a time and times and the dividing of time.
Daniel 7:25

"Hey, look!" Jesse points toward the sign next to the roadway.

Brock peers up at the giant billboard—a picture of Maitreyas dressed in a white robe with a gold sash, standing and smiling with his palms held open next to his sides. The caption reads "SHARING IS CARING." Black spray paint defaces the mural with the word "ANTICHRIST" and then signed "RAD."

"Looks like we may have some friends in this town!" Jesse laughs as the three men pass the sign.

Brock recalls the image of Maitreyas in a TV interview. *"Without sharing there can be no righteousness; without righteousness there can be no peace and security; without peace and security there can be no golden age. . . ."*

"I wonder what RAD stands for?" asks Arturo.

****

The three men tread through the streets of the small town perched on a bluff overlooking a river. As they enter the commercial district, Brock notices someone rummaging through a dumpster behind a shop. He can see himself digging through rotten garbage looking for something to eat. *How humiliating to have to resort to scrounging for food,* he grumbles to himself.

A woman wheels an office chair past them that is filled with stacks of clothes with hangers and tags still attached. Another man is close behind her carrying an armload of shoe boxes.

Looters.

They stop at an intersection where Western-style buildings line both sides of the street.

Armed with knives and axes, people kick down doors and break windows, grabbing food, shoes and clothing, anything they can carry. It reminds Brock of the food riots following the financial collapse; people were starving and too desperate to fear bullets so they pillaged stores and businesses searching for something to eat.

Brock adjusts the strap on the duffle bag over his shoulder. "We should split up and try to find some food."

"Wouldn't that be like stealing?" Arturo asks.

"I think it's okay since this is a crisis." Brock adds, "Let your conscience be your guide."

Brock looks up at the green street sign with white letters. "Let's say we meet back here in about an hour? If you get lost just remember the corner of Placer and Main."

The three men scatter in different directions.

Dumpster diving is fresh in Brock's thoughts so he walks along the back of a building. Although he rebels at the idea he'd heard of grocery stores throwing out perfectly good food if the containers were damaged or past the expiration date. *Maybe I'll get lucky and find something.*

He nears a dumpster and sees a form sleeping next to the brown metal so he decides to keep walking; he doesn't want to disturb the person who may be guarding his territory.

Leaving the alley he crosses the road to the intersection of Quartz and Main Street. He glances up at the stenciled lettering, "World Union Reserve Bank," with the logo of a gold pyramid inside a circle above the door of a crumpled brick building. He notices a poster board lying face up on a pile of glass: "Accepting stocks, bonds, gold and other precious metals and jewels, currency instruments and notes in exchange for American Union sovereigns."

How weird, he thinks. *Since the World Union has implemented the credits, there is nothing of value in the bank to steal.*

He peers through the broken glass; it looks like a normal bank with teller stations and offices. A large poster with a pyramid symbol catches his attention on the back wall: "WARNING: It is forbidden to deface or destroy a Supreme Credit. It is the most sacred of all instruments."

He remembers the pyramid on the back of the old American dollar bill. *Annuit Coeptis Novus Ordor Seclorum*—Latin for "Announcing the birth of New World Order." The eye of Osiris hovered over the unfinished capstone of the pyramid, meaning it was unfinished until the Old World Order was destroyed and replaced with the New World Order.

Yup. He looks at the closed capstone of the pyramid. *They've finally succeeded in creating their New World Order.*

As he steps back into the street he recalls Jesse telling him the pyramid symbol was sacred to the occultists because it was the burial place of Osiris.

Brock notices people running in and out of a store

with a sign above the doorway: "Golden Food Mart."

He quickens his pace.

The glass doors are shattered, but a small plastic sign is still attached to the outside wall: "Store hours: Gaiaday—Joviday—closed Solday."

Gaiaday? Have they implemented the new time laws? Before he was arrested the World Union had called for a five-day calendar week to be put into place. The first day would be called Gaiaday (Monday), second day Monsday (Tuesday), third day Marsday (Wednesday), fourth day Joviday (Thursday) and the fifth day Solday (Friday). The only logical reason Brock figured for their changing the time was to eliminate God's seven-day creation week, thus getting rid of the seventh-day Sabbath and Sunday, the Lord's Day, the two days on which Christians and Jews worshipped.

He enters the market, jostled by others, glass crunching under his shoes. The shelves are empty; papers and cardboard litter the floor. After the earthquake people probably swarmed the store stripping the shelves bare like locusts in a biblical plague.

He views the empty shelves and crates of the produce department—ransacked. Small signs taunt him along the fruit and vegetable islands: "oranges, 20 credits each. . . .apples, 30 credits each. . . ."

His fingers search under empty crates for at least a stray grape but find nothing.

He kneels down and looks under the island. Spotting something behind one of the island cart wheels he stretches his hand underneath until he reaches the red round fruit. He picks it up and stuffs it in his bag.

Back on his feet, he combs through the grocery lanes for food. The aisle of canned vegetables is empty so he keeps walking. Stepping over packages of cloth diapers, he moves to toiletries and cosmetics where he finds a small box marked "BABY SOAP" and a round silver tube and sticks them in his duffle bag.

Discouraged, he exits the store; it's been almost an hour. He hopes Jesse and Arturo had better luck than he did.

Walking through the alley, he hears a whimpering noise coming from behind the dumpster.

He hurries over to find a teen sitting down; his dark sunken eyes stare back at him. The boy's skin is covered with open sores, and his skeletal frame reminds Brock of the victims of the Nazi concentration camps during World War II.

Brock feels deep compassion for the boy and wonders when he'd eaten last.

Without hesitating, he pulls out the red fruit from his bag. "Here."

He sees a faint sparkle in the boy's eyes as his bony hand takes the apple.

Swallowing the lump in his throat Brock continues on.

****

Jesse stands on the street corner with a box tucked under his arm. His face lights up when he sees Brock. "Hey!"

Brock nods. "Where's Arturo?" Just then he sees a white baseball cap and pair of black, baggy shorts bouncing up the street toward them; a dark smudge is on Arturo's mouth, and sunglasses shade his eyes.

Brock stares at the white plastic bag draped over Arturo's arm. "Let's go somewhere and see what we got."

****

Jesse drops the sealed box onto the asphalt.
"What'd you get?" Arturo asks excitedly.

"Not sure. I found a store down the street that was ransacked so I headed to the back. This guy was carrying a case of soda and boxes. I guess I scared him because he dropped everything and ran."

Brock pulls out his knife from the duffle bag then kneels beside the box. The box is light so he's thinking it's a box of potato chips.

With a couple of slices through the packing tape, he peels back the cardboard: twelve 6.5-ounce boxes of mac and cheese dinners.

"Good job, Jesse!"

Arturo frowns. "How we supposed to eat that? We don't have anything to cook it with."

"Don't you worry," Brock assures him. "We'll figure it out later. Now let's see what you got."

Arturo sets the plastic bag on the ground and pours out the contents: a half bag of potato chips, two half-empty bottles of water, a flashlight, a plastic lighter, a CD and an opened package of chocolate chip cookies.

"Wow! I'm impressed."

Brock picks up the flashlight and switches the On button. Nothing—dead batteries.

Jesse grins. "Arturo, where did you find all that stuff?"

"All the stores I went to were looted so I decided to head back when I saw a car buried in debris from the earthquake. That's when I got an idea—I used to stash food in my truck."

Brock looks at the compact disc. Its cover has a picture of an elongated skull with flames spelling the title: Coneheads.

"So what's the CD for?"

"I don't know. . .I just thought it was cool."

Brock chuckles. "I guess you got over your fear of stealing."

"No, it's just that the car was totally smashed. I doubt the owners will be back. So, dude, what'd you get?"

Brock looks down at the green duffle bag as an image of the starving teen by the dumpster appears in his head. "Uh, sorry, guys. . .I struck out."

****

Their bellys full of chips and cookies washed down with warm water, the men walk along Main Street.

Up ahead, a man grunts as he pushes a red, plastic shopping cart.

"I have an idea." Brock drops the duffle off his shoulders, unzips it and pulls out a white box. "You guys wait here."

"BACK OFF!" the man yells, waving a knife.

"Whoa!" Brock steps back. "I don't want to steal your food. I was hoping to trade with you."

The man looks over Brock's shoulder at Jesse and Arturo.

"I *said* back off! Don't come any closer!"

Brock stands firm. "What will you trade for a box of mac and cheese?" He shakes the noodles as he holds the box up for the man to see.

The expression on the man's face suddenly changes; he lowers the knife.

"Hmm." He stares at the box. "My kids sure do like macaroni and cheese."

Brock glances at the white cans with black lettering stacked in the basket.

"How about two cans of chili for a box of mac and cheese?"

The man is thinking.

"No—one box for one can."

"But"—Brock dons his negotiator face—"one box of mac and cheese will feed two kids."

The man thinks long and hard. "How many of them boxes did you say you have?"

Brock smiles. "How many do you want?"

"Okay, how about five boxes of mac and cheese for seven cans of whatever you want."

Now it's Brock's turn to decide.

"If you raise it to eight cans we'll have a deal."

"Deal."

"Hold on." Brock runs over and pulls out four more boxes of the pasta dinners then hurries back to the man.

"Here." He hands the man the stack of boxes then selects eight cans of food from the cart.

Brock grins at Jesse and Arturo. "I hope you guys like chili!"

CHAPTER

11

*For God hath not given us the spirit of fear; but of power,
and of love, and of a sound mind.*
2 Timothy 1:7

"JESSE!" a man's voice calls from behind.

Brock stops and turns his head to see a tall man in dark blue mechanics coveralls hurrying up the street toward them. As the man nears, he recognizes him as the inmate from across the hall, the one with the saggy skin and yellow teeth.

"Big Al!" Jesse grins. "You made it!"

"Yeah!"

A gas station smell accompanies Big Al as he joins them.

"Hey, dude, how'd you get rid of your bracelet?"

"Huh? Oh." Big Al grabs his bare wrist and rubs it. "It was easy. I found a can of motor oil in a gas station, greased it up and slipped it right off."

A loud voice suddenly erupts. "WOE TO HIM!"

Brock turns toward the sound. A group of people are gathering around a long-haired, gray-bearded man standing on the street corner.

"Let's go check him out!" Arturo says.

"See you later!" Big Al takes off in the opposite

direction.

The men hustle toward the man dressed in a tattered, dark brown shirt and brown pants.

"WOE TO HIM who has come in His name, saying, he is the Christ; he has deceived many. His time is short. Very soon he shall be thrown alive into the lake of fire that God has prepared for him."

"WOE TO YOU who call evil good, and good evil, that put darkness for light, and light for darkness. Your name shall be blotted out of the holy books. You shall be cast into the flame which shall burn on the great judgment. Your evil deeds shall be your torment. You shall cry out and lament in the invisible waste in the bottomless fire and burn forever. . . ."

The crowd listens closely to the man's words. He reminds Brock of the two prophets who prophesied from the Wailing Wall in Jerusalem.

An attractive girl in her mid-twenties catches Brock's eye. Her skin is milky white, and a long black braid falls down the middle of her back. *Earth angel,* Brock says to himself. *What a lovely vision for sore eyes.*

Standing next to her is a black-haired boy around fourteen years old.

Probably her brother, Brock assumes. He notices a set of numbers on the boy's forearm and is curious as to what they mean. He remembers an image of the Jews who were tattooed by the Nazis during the Holocaust.

The bearded man shouts, "There is darkness and there is light! The light shall overcome the darkness. Open your eyes and turn from darkness to the light and from the power of Satan to God that you may receive forgiveness of your sins.

"Jesus of Nazareth is the light; he that believes in Him shall not walk in darkness, but shall have the light of eternal life."

The man peers over the crowd searching the faces as though he is looking for someone.

His eyes stop on Jesse.

"This is the message I hear from Him who sent me and declare to you." He pauses then proceeds. "The light dwells in you for all to see for the glory of the Lord rises and shines upon you.'"

Jesse's eyes widen.

The bearded man's gaze sweeps from Jesse to Brock to Arturo then back to Jesse.

"There were four of you; one has fallen. Rejoice! He has called on His Name, and the Lord has heard Him."

Cornelius? Brock is astonished. He recalls the riddle the prison guard spoke. "Four of you will be tried by fire. . .two will fall. . . .'

The bearded man's crystal blue eyes turn toward Brock.

The air is electrifying. Inhaling deep, Brock's heart feels as if it's slamming against his ribcage.

Raising his hand, the bearded man points his finger at Brock's chest. In a clear tone he announces, "God has chosen you. 'Follow the iron snake to where the bear flows with gold. . . .'"

Brock's mouth drops open. *That was the last part of the riddle.*

"CLEAR THE STREETS! LOOTERS AND RIOTERS WILL BE SHOT!" a voice booms over a megaphone. "CLEAR THE STREETS!"

The three men watch as a white military vehicle heads toward them. People disperse in all directions.

****

The sound of water rushing over rocks soothes Brock's soul as he descends along the narrow path to the river bed; Arturo and Jesse are in tow. The smell of nature rushes past his nostrils and fills his lungs. Scattered under the trees are various shelters made up of tents, tarps and tin. Crimson rocks line the river bottom like a fish aquarium filled with colored gravel.

Brock thinks back to when the two prophets responded to the World Union's slaughtering of Christians and Jews by turning the water into blood. *"If it's blood you want,"* they said, *"you shall have blood to drink."*

Arturo interrupts his thoughts. "I wonder why homeless people always hang out at rivers."

Brock's gaze moves to the green nylon tent situated under a tree next to a black truck. "Because of the water."

"What's the big deal about water?"

"Because you can't survive without water. Have you ever heard of the three three's?"

"No."

"You can live three minutes without air, three days without water and three weeks without food."

"Three weeks without food? Man, I can't handle three hours without food."

"There's one more three, but it applies in certain conditions; you can live three hours without shelter."

Arturo is quiet for a minute. "Oh, you mean like in freezing weather or a blizzard or something."

"Yep."

"So how come you know that?"

"I've read many books on survival."

"Cool."

****

"This looks like a good spot." Brock slides the duffel bag off his shoulder and lets it drop to the ground next to a fallen tree.

"Good," says Arturo. "I'm hungry. When we gonna eat?"

"Not so fast—we need to make camp first. Arturo, you collect some wood for a fire and pine needles, and, Jesse—." Brock notices Jesse's face is drenched with sweat and contorted as if he's in pain. "Never mind, Jesse. You go rest. I'll go to the river and get some rocks."

Arturo frowns. "What're the pine needles for?"

"To keep the bugs away and for bedding."

"Oh."

Jesse hobbles over and rests against a tree while Arturo carries armfuls of pine straw and wood and piles them up. Brock hauls rocks to and from the river bank and arranges them in a circle then spreads the pine straw evenly over the ground in front of the fallen log. He pulls out a box of mac and cheese from the duffle bag and hollers to Jesse, "I'll be right back."

"Where you going?"

"To one of those camps to see if I can barter this for something to cook our dinner in."

"I wanna go! Let me go!" Arturo begs.

Brock calls out to Jesse, "What do you think?"

"Sure, let him go."

Brock hands over the white box to Arturo. "We need a cooking pot—and try to get some utensils. Do you think you can handle it?"

Arturo's face beams. "Sure. . .it'll be a cinch."

As Arturo walks away from camp he sticks the box inside the plastic grocery bag dangling from his wrist.

About thirty minutes later Brock hears the shuffle of feet. He sees Arturo's shoulders stooped forward, and he's staring at the ground.

Brock's heart sinks; he knew he should have gone himself.

"No luck, eh?"

Arturo's hand goes into the grocery bag and re-appears with a small dented cooking pot.

Brock's face lights up. "You got a pot?! So why the glum look on your face?"

"I did what you said and asked them if they wanted to trade the mac and cheese for some stuff to cook with. This dude, he was interested at first, but then he wanted to know what else was in my bag. When he saw my Conehead CD, he said no deal unless I included the CD, so I ended up trading the CD for a pot and three spoons."

Brock smiles and nods. "Good job!"

"Yeah, I guess so."

"Who cares about the CD? You can't play it anyway."

Jesse stands and brushes pine needles from the seat of his blue jeans. "I'll make dinner."

Brock fishes out three cans of chili and a box of mac and cheese from the duffle bag and tosses them to Jesse.

His fingers disappear into the duffle again and reappear with a small box.

He strips out of his aqua polo shirt and khaki-colored shorts.

In his boxers and T-shirt he turns toward the cascading water.

"Dude, what's that?"

"Soap."

"Soap? Where did you get soap?"

"Back in town. . .you guys are welcome to use it if you want."

"So what else you stashing?"

"I'm *not* stashing anything. Go ahead and look."

With a mischievous grin on his face, Arturo tugs back the zipper and feels inside the bag, shoving the contents around. His hand slips into a side pocket.

"What's this?" He pulls out a shiny silver tube. He pops the lid off. "LIPSTICK!" He bursts out laughing.

Brock feels his temperature rise and his face flush; he'd forgotten all about the lipstick. He knew how expensive makeup was so he thought maybe he could barter it for something.

Jesse laughs too. "Brock, is there something you want to tell us?"

"Ha, ha, very funny." Brock shakes his head and turns toward the river.

****

The aroma of flavored spices delights Brock's senses as he approaches the camp. Feeling refreshed, he changes out of his wet clothes and into Frank's blue-and-white Hawaiian flowered swim shorts and white T-shirt. He spreads out his underclothes on a tree branch to dry.

Black smoke coils upward into the fading sky from the crackling fire. Arturo sits cross-legged watching Jesse mix the red beans into the cheese-covered pasta then separates the food into three cans. Jesse pushes a spoon into each can then says a prayer of thanks before the three men devour their meal.

The sun vanishes behind the cathedral of pines. A symphony of embers pops as the curling smoke melds with the warm night air. The reddish glow illuminates their faces as the men sit with their backs against the log and stare at the glowing flames fighting their way upward, striving to spread their light into the ink-black night.

Boom. . .boom. . .boom!

"What's that banging noise?" asks Jesse.

Arturo groans. "It sounds like the Coneheads!"

"So much for a nice, peaceful evening."

Boom. . .boom. . .boom!

"It's ironic," Jesse says. "Last night we were running from a fire, and tonight we're huddled around one."

"Yeah. It's a good thing that angel let us out," Arturo adds.

Brock thinks back to the prison fire.

"What makes you think the guard was an angel?" asks Jesse.

"'Cuz Cornelius said so. I bet that prophet dude was an angel too."

"Arturo, not everybody is an angel."

"Then how come he knew about Cornelius?"

"Because he was a prophet, that's why—that's what they do, prophesy!"

Arturo shrugs. "I still think he was an angel."

With the stick in his hand Jesse stokes the fire sending a trail of sparks into the air. "I wonder what he meant by 'follow the iron snake to where the bear flows with gold'?"

"The iron snake is a railroad track," Arturo says.

Brock's ears perk up. *A railroad track?*

"Arturo, what makes you think the iron snake is a railroad track?"

"There's a video game called 'The Iron Serpent,' and on level three you have to cross the railroad tracks that turn into snakes."

Jesse laughs out loud. "I guess you'd have to be into video games to know that! So, Arturo, what does 'the bear that flows with gold' mean? Is there a video game for that too?"

"I don't know what it means. Maybe the bear is a gold

statue or something?"

Brock ponders the riddle. *"Follow the railroad tracks to where the bear flows with gold." Makes sense,* he tells himself. *But what does the rest of it mean?*

Jesse turns his attention to Brock. "Brock, you heard the prophet. He said the Lord has chosen you—"

"No, not me; he must have been mistaken."

Jesse shakes his head. "I don't think he made a mistake."

Brock stares into the fire. "Why would God want anything to do with me?" His voice turns to a low whisper. "After all, I denied Him."

"Why did you deny Him?"

Brock shifts uneasily, searching for an answer. *Why did he deny Jesus and agree to take Maitreyas's mark?*

In a low solemn voice he confesses, "I was afraid of going to hell."

"Why did you think you were going to hell?"

"Because I wasn't right with God—I sinned—"

"We all sin—"

"No." Brock turns his gaze from the fire to Jesse's face. "You don't understand. I willfully sinned. I knew it was wrong, but I convinced myself that as long as I repented it would be okay. I guess you could say I was one of those Christians Mario referred to as 'those who talked the talk but didn't walk the walk.'"

Arturo pipes up. "Dude, what'd you do that was so bad?"

Brock breathes deep then exhales. "I slept with my girlfriend. . .among other things."

"What's wrong with that? Everyone does it. Marriage is for making babies." He snickers.

"Arturo, it's called fornication," Jesse says. "And God has forbidden having sex outside of marriage. I used to think the same thing, that it was okay, but Scripture says it's not—that the body *is not* for fornication but for the Lord and the Lord for the body, that when two people are joined together they become one flesh just as when we are joined to the Lord in one spirit" [1 Corinthians 6: 13-16].

Jesse turns back to Brock. "Did you worship Maitreyas's image and take his mark?"

"No. I was supposed to go down to the execution yard and bow down to Maitreyas's statue. But the bailiff stuck me in a cell, and I guess he forgot about me."

Jesse's face lights up. "Brock! The Bible says that those who worship the beast or his image and take his mark will be lost. You didn't do any of those things!"

"No, but I might as well have. The Bible also says those who deny Jesus before man He will deny before God" [Matthew 10:33].

"Yes, it does say that, but I think if you repent you will be forgiven. Remember Peter? He denied Jesus three times, and Jesus forgave him."

"Jesse is right, dude. Cornelius said the same thing, that if you repent God will forgive you as long as you haven't taken the mark."

For the first time in a long while Brock feels a glimmer of hope.

"So you think I still have a chance? I mean, for Jesus to forgive me?"

"Yes. All you have to do is repent and ask for forgiveness."

The glimmer of hope is suddenly drenched with doubt.

"But even if He does forgive me I don't think I can go through with it, Jesse. I'm so weak. I have such fear." He reaches up and rubs the front of his neck. "I just can't imagine getting my head chopped off. . .and what about the pain?"

"Fear is not from God; it's from the devil. And, besides, aren't fifteen seconds of pain better than an eternity in hell? Just put your faith and trust in the Lord to get through it. The reward will be worth it. I know—suppose you're up there on your knees at the guillotine. Instead of thinking about that blade crashing down on your neck, visualize being on your knees before Jesus and He's placing a golden crown on your head. . . ."

Brock turns his gaze back to the orange and yellow flickering flames. He recalls the story of Peter. Jesus warned Peter he would deny Him three times before the rooster crowed. Peter protested and said even if he had to die he would never deny Jesus. The third time Peter denied Jesus a rooster crowed. When Jesus looked at him, Peter felt such remorse and wept bitterly.

Trembling, Brock tries to swallow, but his mouth is dry. Tears flow down his cheeks as sorrow fills his heart.

"I. . .I want to ask Jesus to forgive me."

Burying his face in his hands his words are muffled. "Dear God. . .I am so sorry I have sinned against You. Please forgive me for denying You. . .please forgive me for sinning willfully. I. . .I knew it was wrong. . . ."

Brock takes in a deep breath then continues. "Please take this anger and hatred away from me that I have toward my dad. I forgive him for all the things he did to me, Mom and Sarah."

His eyes closed, he moves his hands away from his face. "I have such fear, Lord God. Please take this fear away from me and replace it with strength and courage to face persecution and death if it is Your will. And please give me another chance, Lord, like You did Peter. I beg for Your mercy and forgiveness, in Jesus' name, amen."

"Amen!" Jesse and Arturo say together.

Brock wipes the tears from his face. The fire has burned down to a small glowing ember. He feels peace as a heavenly light pierces the dark empty void of his soul. The tightness in his chest dissipates as the chains of bondage are loosened, and fear, anger and hatred scurry away like two cockroaches fleeing from the light.

Such as sit in darkness and in the shadow of death, being bound in affliction and iron; because they rebelled against the words of God, and contemned the counsel of the most High: Therefore he brought down their heart with labour; they fell down, and there was none to help. Then they cried unto the Lord in their trouble, and he saved them out of their distresses. He brought them out of darkness and the shadow of death, and brake their bands in sunder.
Psalm 107:10-14

CHAPTER

12

"Don't look!" Jesse whispers as the three men walk downtown. "A couple of UPs are staring at us."

Union police? Brock tenses.

"Where?" he whispers, looking straight ahead.

"They're in the parking lot on the right."

Brock looks out of the corner of his eye. Two black uniformed officers jump into a white sports utility vehicle.

A wave of hysteria races through his core. *The prison must have warned the local law enforcement to be on the lookout for escapees.*

Keep calm, he tells himself and tightens the grip on the duffle bag strap.

His pace quickens till they pass the brown block building obstructing their view from the police.

"RUN!" Brock cries and forces his legs full speed ahead.

The three men bolt down the street, turn right at the intersection and duck into an alley.

Brock sees a metal trash dumpster. Without a thought he speeds to the bin and hurls himself over the side. Cardboard boxes squeak and groan as he sinks into an ocean of trash.

"Gross!" Arturo says as he and Jesse climb in. "It smells like someone died in here."

Jesse's breaths come hard and quick. "Do you think

they're after us?"

"Hope not," Brock says. Crouching low he strains his ears as his heart thumps rapidly against his chest.

"UGH." Arturo utters a loud, deep, guttural sound, followed by a sudden shifting of boxes.

"Be quiet and stay down." Brock's elbow jabs Arturo in the ribs.

"But. . . ."

Gritting his teeth Brock repeats, "Be quiet!"

The men freeze on hearing the sound of gravel popping under rubber tires. An SUV snails its way by the alley.

Brock holds the air in his lungs.

Gradually the vehicle passes and vanishes down the street.

"That was close." Brock throws his legs over the metal side and drops to the ground; Jesse and Arturo climb out of the trash bin after him.

Brock glares at Arturo. "Are you crazy? You could have got us killed."

"But I saw something." Arturo's voice is innocent. "If you don't believe me look for yourself."

Shaking his head, Brock peers into the garbage container. "What? I don't see anything but trash."

"Under there." Arturo points toward the piece of cardboard splattered with red.

Leaning over the side Brock pokes at the cardboard where hordes of flies have amassed. A severed hand rolls over with a white bracelet attached.

"Ugh!" A horrified look shrouds Brock's face.

"I told you so!" Arturo defends himself.

Brock shudders as he envisions the prisoner chopping off his own hand. In a few seconds alarm bells go off in his head that they are in grave danger being so close to the tracking device. "We gotta get out of here and quick!"

****

The men race through back alleyways and parking lots, putting distance between them and the tracking bracelet.

"Look!" Jesse points up ahead. "Railroad tracks!"

"Follow the iron snake to where the bear flows with gold. . . ."

The men step off the asphalt and turn onto the dirt road and follow the tracks through faded antique warehouses and large loading ramps.

Brock glances at a two-story Victorian-style building. A sign posted above the door reads "Pine Hills Railroad Depot," and behind the depot is a small rusted steam locomotive.

The men pass the railroad station and continue to follow the iron rails along the top of the river canyon. Massive Ponderosa pines and vertical granite slabs adorn the scenic view; it reminds Brock of a painting his aunt Millie had hanging in her living room.

"What's that?" Arturo interrupts his thoughts.

Brock looks at several black containers stored on sidetracks surrounded by a chain link fence.

"It looks like a railroad yard," he replies.

Jesse stops abruptly. "Listen. . . ."

Brock stops. He tries to listen over the birds chirping and the river rushing below. Then he hears an undeniable rhythmic whump-whump-whump sound of a helicopter in the distance.

"Run for cover!"

Arturo lunges toward an open container. "Let's hide in there!"

Brock peeks over Arturo's shoulder into the boxcar. Rows of metal shackles are welded to the inside walls. Horrid memories flood his head as he recalls his boxcar prison and what these containers were used for.

"No!" he steps back.

"Why not?" Arturo argues.

Whump-whump-whump. The helicopter gets louder as it approaches.

"The shed! Over there!" Jesse yells.

Brock's gaze follows Jesse's fingers to the leaning structure that's no bigger than a chicken coop.

The men pile inside the black space slamming the door behind them.

Gasping for air Arturo whispers, "I wonder if they saw us."

Whump-whump-whump. The helicopter sounds as if it's hovering overhead.

Brock brushes away a sticky, silk web from his face. He half expects a black widow spider to crawl from the darkness and lock its venomous fangs into his skin.

He can barely breathe as he waits. Slowly his eyes adapt to the dark. A blue towel is nailed over a small window; cobwebs and carved initials plaster the wood walls; crumpled candy and chip wrappers litter the dirty floor. Three blue plastic milk crates were flipped upside down, and a white candle is used as a centerpiece on one of them.

Jesse puts his hand out. "I hear something."

Brock listens over the blades cutting through the air and hears gravel snap as a vehicle moves slowly along the railroad tracks.

A car. . .someone is coming. . . . Anxiety grips him.

Several sets of boots crunch on the gravel. He hears a grinding sound as someone slides a boxcar door open.

"ALL CLEAR!" A man's deep voice penetrates the

train yard.

The boots go from boxcar to boxcar. Brock realizes they are sweeping the train yard looking for someone. *Are they looking for us?*

Sweat drips from his forehead. *Will they search the shed?*

His eyes turn to Arturo whose face is buried in his hands then to Jesse. His eyes are closed, and his lips are moving. *He's praying. I should be doing the same thing. Dear Lord God,* he cries out in his head. *"Please don't let them find us—"*

"IN THERE!" a raspy voice orders.

Brock's jaw clenches and his muscles tighten as he braces for the impact when the shed door is kicked open and they are discovered.

Will they shoot us in the shed? Or will they arrest us and parade us through town before they behead us?

Footsteps scuffle on the gravel.

POP! POP! Two gunshots sound through the train yard, followed by a loud gasp then muffled voices.

Arching his eyebrows, Brock looks from Jesse to Arturo. *Someone has been shot. . .but who?* He sits bewildered, too terrified to move.

The helicopter sounds as if it's ascending into the sky, and then the whirring diminishes over the mountains.

They hear more masculine voices, and then several car doors slam. An engine roars to life and slowly drives away in the direction of town.

Jesse sighs out loud. "I think they're gone."

Jumping to his feet, Brock steps over to the blue towel and tugs the cotton away from the window and peers outside. He sees a body lying face-down next to the tracks, shirtless, wearing a pair of black shorts. Red oozes from the scruffy black hair and down the back of the man's neck. He notices a white bracelet on the man's wrist.

"It's an inmate," he says out loud. "They shot him dead right through the skull. They must have tracked him here; he's wearing a bracelet."

Brock backs away from the window and sits back down on the floor. He thinks about the night Cornelius was shot. "They'll probably be back for the body."

Arturo frowns. "How'd they track that guy if he was in a metal container? I thought the metal made you invisible."

"They probably tracked him until the signal disappeared at the boxcars."

"Boy, that was close," Jesse says. "I thought for sure they were following us."

Silently the men wait in the shed till they hear a vehicle drive up, throw the body into a truck and then drive back toward town.

****

The sun slowly dips behind the mountains blanketing the train yard with darkness.

Sitting with his legs sprawled in front of him on the floor with the duffle bag supporting his back, Brock eats a cold can of chili. Jesse and Arturo sit across from him on the plastic crates.

Arturo sticks his spoon into the empty chili can and sets it on the crate table next to the candle. He pulls out a lighter from his pocket. After igniting the wick he leans back against the wall and stares at the flickering flame.

"That was just too close." Arturo shakes his head. "If we'd a hid in them boxcars we'd a got busted."

He moves his eyes to Brock. "How'd you know, dude?"

"Know what?" Brock drops his spoon into his empty can then sets the can on the floor beside him.

"You know, how did you know not to hide in the boxcars?"

Brock wipes his mouth with the back of his hand. "I guess you could say I had a premonition."

Arturo's eyes open wide. "Really?"

"Well, no, not really," he confesses then grimaces. "The truth is, I loathe them."

"Why? They're just stupid train cars for hauling stuff."

"No, Arturo, those particular train cars were designed and used to haul people to death camps to exterminate them."

"No way! You're kidding, right?"

Brock can tell Arturo doesn't believe him. Most people don't. When he'd try to explain they'd look at him as if he had a third eye on his forehead or was just another crazy conspiracy theorist. But he knew. He'd researched government records and laws and interviewed people who built the boxcars and death camps.

"I was doing a story on them for my newspaper and was going to expose the atrocities the World Union was committing against Christians and Jews when I got arrested.

"You see, Arturo, long before America joined with Canada and Mexico to form the North American Union, they built these camps under the guise of emergency management. They secretly built hundreds of them all over the United States. They were just waiting for martial law to be implemented so they could put their plans into effect.

"One of my sources, John, was a former Central Intelligence Agency (CIA) agent. He admitted to me that he had helped design the plans for many of these camps.

"I also interviewed a satanist who became a Christian. He worked with military planners for the New World Order takeover and told me they planned on brutally raping, torturing and killing those who were taken to the camps. He said they would sit around and discuss how long they could torture a person until the person finally died. They came up with twelve to thirteen days."

"That is just sick." Arturo shakes his head. "I don't get how come God allows that to happen."

"Arturo," Jesse says, joining in the conversation, "nobody said it would be easy. . .in fact, Jesus said it would be very difficult."

"Yeah, I guess so." Arturo's eyes are downcast.

"I know it's hard. That's why we need to pray for strength and courage during these tough times. I think we should pray right now and thank the Lord for bringing us this far."

The men close their eyes and bow their heads.

"Dear Lord Jesus," Jesse starts, "thank You for sparing our lives once again and giving us safe refuge and yet another day. We thank You, Lord.

"Please give us the strength and courage to face those who hate us and persecute us, for we know they hate us because they hated You first.

"We praise Your holy name, the name God has given You which is above every name: that at the name of Jesus every knee should bow and every tongue should confess that Jesus Christ *is* Lord, to the glory of God the Father."

"Grrrrrr."

Brock hears a low animal-like growl. His eyes pop open to find Arturo's and Jesse's eyes are closed. He discounts the noise as some animal outside or his over-active imagination.

"You are the Lamb who was sacrificed, and we thank You for dying on the cross for our sins and rising from the dead. You have redeemed us by Your precious blood that cleanses us from all sin."

Jesse's voice becomes firm. "We will overcome Satan

and his kingdom by the blood of the Lamb—"

"Grrrrrr."

There it is again! Brock's eyes shoot open. The noise is coming from Arturo. His eyes are narrow, the pupils black slits. An unseen supernatural force twists Arturo's face into a grotesque shape.

Brock is stunned by what he sees.

Jesse blurts out loud, "Jesus! Please help Arturo!"

"Jesus?" A deep, sinister tone forces its way out of Arturo's vocal cords as its demonic eyes glare back at Jesse.

Brock forces his mind to try to comprehend what is happening. Something is inside Arturo. He's heard of this before but has never witnessed it with his own eyes. The hairs on his arms stand on end as chills slide up and down his spine.

"Jesus cannot help Arturo, for it is I who am his protector and he is my servant. He belongs to me! I will flog him and eat his soul for all eternity!"

The menacing voice laughs. "Greater is Lucifer than Jesus, for he is the only morning star, the one true son of the dawn!"

Speechless, Jesse stares back at Arturo.

"Who. . . ," Brock stammers, "who. . .are you?"

Arturo's head swings around to face Brock.

"I was formed by the hands of Lucifer. I am the keeper of the serpent's head—the spirit of old. I am the anointed one who molests your mind and your dreams. I am the one who guides you to the water of life; I am the one who quenches your thirst!"

The one who quenches your thirst? Brock feels his skin crawl as he remembers the dream he had a few nights ago. *Was this demon in his dream?*

"In the name of Jesus, THE LORD REBUKE YOU, EVIL SPIRIT!" Jesse speaks with great authority. "I

COMMAND YOU TO LEAVE!"

The demon turns toward Jesse. "You cannot cast me out. I am the prince and ruler of the legion, and all who see my face bow down before me for I am like god." He snickers. "It was I who forced the nails into Jesus' hands, and it is I who will visit your sleep tonight and impregnate your thoughts with lust—"

"Evil spirit." Jesse's eyes blaze with fire. "You were defeated at the cross, and what comes out of your mouth is nothing but lies because you are like your father the devil, the father of lies. In the name of JESUS, I COMMAND YOU TO LEAVE!"

Arturo's eyes roll back into his head, and his body falls off the plastic crate to the floor.

Shaken, Brock doesn't move. It's as though he's waiting for Arturo to sit up and his head to start spinning around in circles.

Jesse places his hand on Arturo's shoulder. "Arturo?" His hand gently nudges him. "Arturo, are you okay?"

Arturo moves his head and opens his eyes. His face is no longer contorted, and his eyes appear to be normal.

"What happened?" Arturo sits up.

"You had a demon, and he manifested," Jesse replies.

"What? No way, dude. . .a demon?" His eyes widen; his voice shakes.

"Yes, a demon.

"Arturo, have you ever been involved in witchcraft or played the Ouija board?"

Arturo hesitates.

"Or maybe had your palms read or talked to a psychic—anything that might invite an evil spirit in?"

"No, I don't think so. Uh, wait. . .yes, I did. I forgot about it till just now."

"What'd you do?" Brock stares hard at Arturo.

"Uh, played with a Ouija board. . .but it's kind of a long story."

"We're not going anywhere," says Jesse.

Arturo moves back to the plastic crate then pulls the ball cap off his head and holds it in both hands. "When I was thirteen, we moved here from Italy. I went to a new school and was bullied because I didn't know English very well. I didn't have any friends, and I was very lonely.

"I remember watching a movie about a kid who was picked on in school just like me. Anyway, he became a wizard. He would cast spells on the kids that were mean to him and made them his servants. I thought this was pretty cool so I learned how to cast spells on the internet watching videos.

"Nothing happened. Then I discovered you could talk to spirits on a Ouija board so I talked my mom into buying me one. She thought it was just an innocent game." He shakes his head.

"Most parents do," Brock says.

Jesse nods in agreement.

"Anyway, my little sister and I tried to work the board for about three days. Finally the triangular-shaped pointer thing began to move from letter to letter on the board. We saw only garbled messages at first. My sister got scared of the board and refused to play it with me anymore so I played it by myself. The first couple of days, the little pointer thing wouldn't move. I kept trying and didn't give up. Finally the pointer seemed to come to life and moved quickly from letter to letter. It was crazy! I would ask it questions, and it answered me. Soon a spirit revealed itself to me and said it would be my friend and would guide me and protect me. I remember thinking at the time that it was pretty cool, you know, having a spirit guide.

"Then one day my dad saw a ghost in the house and

chased it out the window. My little sister ratted on me and said it came from my Ouija board. That's when Dad tossed it in the trash."

Arturo places his cap on his head backward and folds his arms over his chest.

"So then what happened?" Jesse asks.

"Nothing. That was it. I never talked to my spirit guide again. End of story."

"I never wanted to go near a Ouija board." Brock shifts his weight on the floor. "I knew a girl with one, and it freaked me out."

"Arturo," Jesse says, "your spirit guide was an evil spirit, and he didn't leave you when your dad tossed the board in the trash. When you dabble in the occult, like playing with a Ouija board, the Charlie, Charlie, or the Ice Bucket Challenge, having your palms read, astrology, horoscopes and even playing some video games—all of these things can open doors for evil spirits to enter. And the Bible forbids it."

After a few minutes of silence Brock speaks up. "So, Arturo, when did you become a Christian?"

"When did I become a Christian?" Arturo's eyes narrow. "I have *always* been a Christian. I was born a Christian."

"Nobody is *born* a Christian, Arturo," Jesse says. "It's a choice you have to make. You have to accept and believe in your heart that Jesus is the Christ and that God raised Him from the dead" [Romans 10:9].

"Well, this may sound funny to you guys, but I know I'm a Christian because my mom said I was."

CHAPTER

13

I beheld, and, lo, that horn made war against the saints,
and prevailed over them.
Daniel 7: 21

The low humming of a vehicle engine arouses Brock from a blissful sleep. Anxiety shoots through his blood vessels; he feels the sudden threat of danger.

"Jesse. . .Arturo. . .wake up!" Brock whispers. "Someone's outside!"

"Hello? Is anyone in there?" A male voice speaks from outside the shed. "This is the police."

The police? An overpowering terror chokes Brock.

"Yes," Jesse answers and scrambles to his feet. "Hang on a minute."

"Jesse, what the heck are you doing?" Brock's brows draw together.

"I'm gonna try to get rid of him."

"How?"

"Don't know. . .just pray."

Jesse steps to the door; his hair is matted in back.

The door swings open.

A blast of daylight pours into the shelter. Brock squints and sees a tall, chubby, American Union police officer with his hand on his holster ready to draw his gun. By the look on his face it's obvious the young man wasn't expecting anyone in the shed.

The cop puffs out his chest and makes his face stern. "What're you doing in there?"

"Oh, uh, we just crashed here for the night—"

"Who's *we*?"

Jesse steps aside. "Me, my stepson and my nephew."

The young man eyeballs Arturo then Brock.

Brock nods at the officer clad in a black uniform and matching beret. He hopes he buys Jesse's phony story.

"You see, officer, we were headed to the Bay Area when the earthquake struck, and we got stranded in town. We thought we'd try to thumb a ride back to Reno when we got lost so we crashed here for the night."

"Uh. . .oh, I see." Relief shows on the cop's face, and his body relaxes. He moves his hand away from his firearm and takes a step back. "You guys be on the lookout for some escaped convicts in this area."

"Escaped convicts?" Jesse makes his voice sound surprised.

"Yes, there was a big fire up at the prison, and some of the prisoners got away."

"Oh, thank you. We sure will."

The officer turns away, and Jesse shuts the door.

"That was close." Brock lets out a long breath.

A vehicle door slams shut. About ten minutes pass, and the sound of the engine continues to purr outside.

Fear inches into the shed as the men wait for the vehicle to leave.

"What are they doing?" Arturo asks. "Are they ever gonna leave?"

Brock jumps to his feet and cracks the door open. His eyes lock onto a white SUV marked POLICE parked near a cluster of granite rocks a short distance away. Two men are in the front seat.

"Not good." Brock snaps the door shut.

"What do you mean 'not good'?" Arturo asks.

"I saw two men in the car; it looked like they were arguing."

Brock hears a car door creak open and then slam shut through the running motor.

He nervously waits.

TAP—TAP—TAP on the wood door.

Slowly Brock pulls the door open. He notices some sort of device in the cop's hand.

"Yes? Is there anything we can do for you, officer?" Brock asks.

"Uh, sorry to bother you fellows, but my partner insists that you show us some ID. If you'll just stick out your right hand, we'll be on our way."

Brock stares at the plastic gun-like device. "Uh. . .what for?"

"So I can scan your ID."

Blood rushes to Brock's head. He feels the same fear he'd felt in his dream when Peter Roma demanded he show him his certificate proving he'd made a sacrifice to Osiris.

His insides tremble. Fear screams at him to run, but his legs won't budge. They feel as if they're cemented in concrete.

Lord God, what should I do?

Have no fear—walk in the Spirit, a voice answers.

Slowly Brock extends his right arm.

The officer directs the device over the back of Brock's hand, and a blue laser light emits. The officer waves the light back and forth then bangs it against his palm a few times then repeats.

Frustrated, the cop scratches his cheeks. "The scanner doesn't seem to be working." He transfers the laser gun to his other hand then points the blue laser light at the back of his right hand. A series of bleeps come from the scanner then the word Maitreyas suddenly appears followed by Nathan Conners and a series of numbers.

The police officer stares at the blue impression for a minute; then the scanner drops to the floor as he fumbles for his gun.

Aiming his firearm at Brock's chest, he takes a step backward.

"Where's God's mark?" the officer demands.

"You mean, the mark of the beast?" Brock boldly declares, "I don't have one."

"You guys just hold it right there." The officer's voice is shaky.

"Smitty! Quick! Come here!" he yells. "I think we found us some resisters!"

The engine shuts off, and a car door slams.

Gun drawn, a medium-sized UP officer takes long strides toward the shed. His short face and under-bite resemble a bulldog.

With cold, bloodshot eyes that show no mercy, Smitty studies Brock, then Jesse and finally Arturo then turns to the young cop. "Now, Nathan, aren't you glad you listened to me?"

"Yeah, Smitty, you were right."

Smitty waves his gun. "Okay, pond scum, hands on your head. Step out of the shed one at a time. Anybody try anything stupid, I'll blast a hole in your brain."

Smitty nudges his gun at Brock's chest.

"You first."

Raising his hands over his head, Brock steps out into the morning light; then Jesse; then Arturo. Smitty directs them toward the chain-link fence that encloses the railroad yard.

"Face the fence and spread your arms and legs," he

hisses.

The three men turn toward the fence.

Brock spread-eagles his legs and soon feels Nathan's chubby hand run along the outside of his shirt and shorts patting him down.

"Now turn around and sit down," Smitty barks, "but keep your hands on top of your head."

Obeying, the three men drop to the ground and sit cross-legged with their hands resting on top of their heads.

Smitty walks over to the SUV leaving Nathan to stand guard. He opens the door and reaches deep inside. A few seconds later he has a phone plastered against his ear and is talking to someone.

Brock dreads what will happen to them. *Will they send us back to prison? Or straight to the guillotine? Or will they just kill us on the spot?*

The car door slams.

Clutching his gun and small notepad and pen, Smitty walks over and shoves the blue pad at Nathan. He whispers something then turns and walks up to the fence and stops in front of Brock with the gun aimed at his chest.

Brock's eyes move to the metal barrel. At any moment this man could shoot him dead.

Smitty glares at Brock. "What is your name?"

"Brock Summers."

Nathan writes on the notepad.

"Who is the Christ?"

Who is the Christ? Brock wasn't expecting this question; he was thinking Smitty would ask him where he worked or lived but not this.

He draws in a deep breath then exhales. He confesses in his clearest voice, "Jesus of Nazareth, the Son of the living God."

Smitty snarls. "Deny Him or you will die."

Deny Jesus? Brock looks at the gun then at the silver, six-pointed star attached to the breast of Smitty's black shirt. He reflects on his court trial and remembers the moment he'd agreed to take Maitreyas's mark. It felt as if someone had stabbed him in the heart and all of his joy had bled out leaving an empty hollow shell.

His gaze moves back to Smitty's face.

"No, I can't. I denied Jesus once before, and I died inside. He has forgiven me, and I have peace—and I will never deny Him again."

"Yeah, yeah, yeah. Save your sob story for someone who cares."

Smitty turns to Jesse. "What is your name, old man?"

"Jesse Chapman."

Nathan moves the pen over the pad of paper, his jowls jiggling like Jell-o with each movement.

"Who is the Christ?"

"You heard him." Jesse smiles confidently. "Jesus is the Christ. He is King of kings and Lord of lords!"

Smitty scowls. "Deny Him or you will die!"

Jesse replies, "Who is a liar but he that denieth that Jesus is the Christ? He is antichrist, that denieth the Father and the Son" [John 2:22].

Smitty's lip curls as he turns toward Arturo.

"What is your name, young man?"

"Arturo Corelli."

Nathan jots on the pad of paper.

"Who is the Christ?"

"Jesus."

"I *can't* hear you."

"I *said* Jesus."

Smitty turns and walks away then stops; he seems to be deep in thought. He slips his gun into the holster. Looking at the ground he peels off his black beret and scratches his gray-buzzed head then replaces it. He walks back over to Arturo.

"Hey, kid." Smitty smiles. "How old are you?"

Brock notices Smitty's demeanor has changed and can tell he is trying to act friendly.

"Nineteen."

"Now I'm sure these fellows have convinced you that Jesus is still floating around somewhere in the clouds. Well, I'm here to tell you Jesus isn't in the clouds at all. You see, he has reincarnated as Peter Roma. Why, just this morning I saw him on TV making a speech in Jerusalem with Lord Maitreyas. Now how can Jesus be in two places at once?"

Arturo's gaze is locked on the ground. "Don't know."

Brock's mind goes to the Holy City. *I wonder what they're doing in Jerusalem.* Before he was arrested Maitreyas made a seven-year peace treaty with Israel that would allow Israel to share the Temple Mount and build the new temple. *I wonder if the temple has been completed yet.*

"Look, Arturo. You have a long life ahead of you. Aren't you tired of running? You had to know that eventually you'd get caught."

Arturo is silent.

"You know what, young man?"

"What?" Arturo continues to stare at the ground.

"You're a very lucky kid because I can help save you."

Brock shakes his head. *The sly old snake.* Smitty reminds him of the serpent who cunningly persuaded Eve to eat the fruit in the Garden of Eden. Only this snake is trying to persuade Arturo to take the mark.

Smitty continues. "They are looking for some young people to join the force. As an officer you will get all kinds of perks, and they feed you real good." He snickers, glancing at Nathan then back to Arturo. "I can put in a word for you."

Arturo lifts his head and looks at Smitty.

"All you have to do is kneel before an image of Lord Maitreyas and say a few words of the Luciferian oath. Then you'll be free to go. It's as simple as that." He turns and starts to walk toward the SUV. "Hold on a minute. . .I'll be right back."

Nathan stands guard.

A blue-gray sparrow hawk flies down from the sky and lands on a tree limb. The bird pushes out his orange-striped breast and looks down on them.

That's strange, Brock says to himself. *That's the same kind of bird that was at Lorraine's execution.*

As Smitty walks back to the fence, Brock notices he has something gold tucked under his arms.

He sets a two-foot gold idol on the ground in front of Arturo—an image of Maitreyas in a prayerful pose.

"There you go—all you have to do now is kneel and repeat some words after me, and then you can go."

"No, Arturo! Don't do it!" shouts Brock.

Smitty scowls as he draws his firearm back out of the holster and steps over to Brock.

Brock flinches. He is sure Smitty is going to put a bullet in his head; instead he clobbers him in the head with the butt of the gun.

He hears a cracking sound at the moment of impact, and a bolt of light flashes before Brock's eyes. A throbbing pain instantly shoots through his head, and blood pours from his nose.

Smitty packs his gun into his holster and walks back over to Arturo.

"Now get on your knees, kid, and bow down to Lord Maitreyas," he demands angrily.

"No! I can't do it." Arturo bursts into tears.

Smitty's face looks like a backed-up volcano ready to unleash its fury. He looks to Nathan. "Go ahead and blow his brains out."

A gasp pushes past Brock's lips. He is horrified.

Nathan drops the notepad on the ground and pulls out his pistol. He steps over to Arturo and plants the tip of the barrel at the back of Arturo's neck.

Tears run down Arturo's face.

"You heard Smitty. Bow to Lord Maitreyas or die!" Nathan orders.

With Nathan's gun planted in the back of Arturo's skull, Arturo tucks his legs under his body and slowly moves on his hands and knees toward the gold statue.

Arturo's lips quiver. "I—"

"No! Don't do it, Arturo—be strong!" Jesse pleads. "Remember what Cornelius said, that your soul will be tormented in hell if you worship the beast and take his mark."

Nathan cocks back the hammer of the gun. "Deny Jesus. . .NOW!"

Arturo's body shakes violently, and his face twists in misery as water gushes from his eyes. "I . . .I. . .deny Jesus," he wails.

"That a boy." Smitty reaches into his pocket and unfolds a piece of paper and holds it out. "Now repeat after me, 'I do solemnly swear. . ."

Arturo raises his arm and wipes his nose and face.

"I. . .I do solemnly swear. . ."

"That I will henceforth be a faithful servant of the most high god Lucif. . . ."

Brock wants to run over and pull Arturo to his feet and slap some sense into him, but he knows it will do no good; he's learned that Satan uses fear to control those who are weak. Instead he turns his head away and blocks out the words from entering into his head. He imagines Arturo's spirit guide is gloating with venomous, malicious satisfaction as Arturo relinquishes his soul to the devil, the red dragon, the serpent of old.

"I accept the secret doctrines," Smitty continues, "the visions, and will seek to communicate with the ascended masters. . ."

Arturo repeats, "I accept the secret doctrines, the visions, and will seek to communicate with the ascended masters. . . ."

Arturo continues to repeat after Smitty: ". . .to a higher state of consciousness. I enter this agreement with the most high god. And I will seal this oath by accepting Lord Maitreyas's name, the mark of his name or his number 666 in my right hand or forehead."

Brock hears the echo of Arturo's amen.

Smitty pulls Arturo to his feet. "There now, was that so bad? Now come with me."

"But you said I could go if I took the oath."

"Not so fast. You can go when headquarters says you can go. Now shut up and come with me."

Dragging his feet, Arturo walks with Smitty to the police car and climbs into the back seat.

What will become of Arturo? Brock wonders. An image suddenly appears in his mind of a sick, skinny teenage boy curled up next to a dumpster. He is dressed in a baggy black shirt and shorts and wears a white baseball cap turned backward. His soulless eyes look up at him. They belong to Arturo.

The door slams, and Smitty walks back to the men.

"Anyone else? How 'bout you?" He looks at Brock with a sardonic grin.

Brock avoids Smitty's eyes and stares at the patch on the sleeve of his uniform. A pyramid surrounded by ten stars embroidered in gold reads "World Union—Novus Ordo Seclorum—A New Order for the Ages."

"I'd rather die a thousand deaths than bow down to the beast."

"Okay, if that's how you feel, we'll be happy to accommodate you."

"How 'bout you, old man?"

"'The man who loves his life will lose it,'" Jesse replies, "'while the man who hates his life in this world will keep it for eternal life'" [John 12:25].

Smitty's face tightens. His hand moves to a holder attached to his belt, and he draws out a straight black stick.

Standing with his legs spread apart he hits the baton against his palm. "Say Christ Maitreyas, old man," he commands.

"I will not." Jesse's voice is firm.

"What's wrong with saying Christ Maitreyas and taking his mark to save yourself?"

"Because Jesus is the only Christ, and those who take Maitreyas's mark will go to hell."

Smitty shakes his head. "Take the oath, and I will release you like I did your friend."

"No, I will not."

Smitty raises the baton in the air. His ropelike veins bulge in his neck, and his face turns crimson. He raises his voice. "I'm gonna give you two seconds to say Christ Maitreyas."

Jesse cowers low against the fence, shielding his face with his arms.

"You do what I say!" Smitty bellows. His arm comes crashing down on Jesse with the stick.

Jesse's hands, forearms and triceps take the brunt of the blows as he makes a futile attempt to defend himself.

Smitty stops.

Brock looks at Jesse's pale face. He looks dazed and is trying to recover from the impact of the beating; a gash appears on his forehead, and blood streams from the bridge of his nose.

"I will have to kill you if you do not change your mind." He shoves his boot into Jesse's side. "Did you hear me?"

"Yes."

"Stupid old fool."

Smitty turns his attention to Brock.

"Say Christ Maitreyas."

Brock sits tight-lipped and covers his head with his forearms.

The officer raises his hand and starts striking Brock with his black stick.

"Where's your Jesus now? Call him to come and save you!"

Every blow sends excruciating pain through Brock like an electrical charge.

Lord! he cries silently. *Please help me. . .please give me strength.*

He remembers a verse: *"I can do all things through Christ who strengthens me."* He repeats this over and over with each strike. *"I can do all things through Christ who strengthens me. . . ."*

Smitty stops.

He walks over and hands the baton to Nathan. The cops take turns beating the men, stopping only to satisfy their thirst with a water bottle retrieved from the SUV. These men have human faces but are no longer human. They behave like animals that pleasure themselves before conquering their kill.

Tongue swollen from dehydration, Brock's body convulses with pain. He glances over at Jesse—curled in a fetal position, beaten to a bloody pulp. As he looks at Jesse he thinks about Jesus and the horrific pain He must have felt at the hands of the Roman soldiers as He was brutally tortured. How He must have labored carrying the wooden cross-beam through the streets of Jerusalem while He was ridiculed and mocked along the way to be crucified. And after all that He'd suffered He still had compassion for His enemies: "Father God, forgive them for they know not what they do."

It suddenly dawns on him: *Maybe this is what Jesus meant when He said, "Take up your cross and follow Me; for whoever will save his life shall lose it: and whoever will lose his life for My sake shall find it?" Come to think of it, all but one of His disciples died a martyr's death.*

Nathan sips from a bottle of water. "How much longer, Smitty? I'm getting tired and hungry."

"Almost done," Smitty answers matter-of-factly.

He pulls out a small canister from his belt and twists the top then walks back to Brock. With one hand he grabs a fistful of Brock's hair and quickly points the container into Brock's eyes and sprays.

"OH!" Brock snaps his head back and shrieks in pain from the horrific burning. His eyes water, and his nose runs. He coughs hard trying to rid his airway of the toxic chemical. Already he feels the irritation permeating his lungs. *Lord God, how much more can I take?*

"On your knees," Smitty demands.

Brock attempts to kneel. His eyes burn, and it feels as if every inch of his body is broken from the beating.

A chubby hand grabs his shirt and pulls him into a kneeling position. Jesse's shoulder brushes against his as the two men kneel side-by-side.

"I am with you," a calm soothing voice rings through the train yard.

Brock feels an electromagnetic power surge envelop his body. He strains to force his eyes open, but his burning lids won't submit.

"It's Jesus!" Jesse whispers. "He is with us!"

"Yes," Brock replies. "I know."

Jesse begins reciting Psalm 23: "The Lord is my shepherd; I shall not want. He maketh me to lie down in green pastures: he leadeth me beside the still waters."

Brock joins in. "He restoreth my soul: he leadeth me in the paths of righteousness for his name's sake. Yea, though I walk through the valley of the shadow of death, I will fear no evil: for thou art with me—"

"If you guys are lucky," snickers Smitty, "you'll die instantly."

Cringing, Brock braces himself. *Will I die instantly? Or will I suffer a slow and agonizing death? Give me strength, Lord. I am weak.*

Brock focuses on Jesus and tries to picture Him on a heavenly throne as the martyrs praise Him dressed in white robes. He sees Cornelius; he sees Lorraine.

"Glory, glory, glory to Jesus!" he whispers. "Holy, holy, holy is Your precious name!" He feels joy in his heart as tears stream down his face. Shortly he will be joining them. "You are King of kings and Lord of—"

Suddenly gunfire erupts.

Bullets whiz toward the two men in lightning speed and ricochet off the wire fence.

Brock feels a horrific pain like a stick of dynamite going off in his shirt pocket. An agonizing grunt escapes his lips as he reels backward against the fence knocking the wind out of him before he falls forward smacking his face hard on the ground. He gasps to fill his lungs with air. The torment is unbearable; it feels like a jack-hammer drilling his chest.

The exploding sound of gunfire has stopped. Smitty and Nathan are talking; they sound so far away.

"What do we do with their bodies, Smitty?" asks

Nathan.

"Headquarters will send someone to pick them up."

Large amounts of adrenaline begin to release in Brock's body making everything in slow motion. It feels as if he's falling into a deep, deep hole. . .their voices are fading. . . .

****

Lying motionless on the ground, Brock slips into a dream state. A bright light hovers over him. The light pours into his body like liquid, starting at the top of his head and flowing to the tips of his toes.

Feeling weightless, he springs to his feet. His memory smacks him back to the moment. Shots were fired, and he fell to the ground. He is sure he was shot, but for some reason he doesn't feel any pain.

Am I dead? he wonders.

His eyes search the ground half-expecting to find his corpse, but it's not there. Then he remembers Jesse and scans the ground for him, but he can't find him either.

An uncanny feeling washes over him. The hairs on his arms stand up straight, and his body's defenses kick into high gear. He spins around toward the boxcars where he sees a dark shadowy figure creeping toward him.

What the—? Brock's muscles tense.

The sinister figure nears him. It stands upright like a man. Its face is grotesque, its outer body black and scaly like a fish, eyes like burning coals of fire.

Keeping his gaze locked on the monster Brock raises his arms to defend himself. He lowers his body into a fighting stance with one foot forward, his shoulders apart, his knees bent.

The creature growls, baring fanged teeth, circling

Brock. In a quick movement it thrusts forward, eyes filled with rage.

Brock uses his limbs to block the evil creature, but the demon is quick and wraps its arms around Brock knocking them both to the ground. The demon sinks his fangs into Brock's neck sending a searing pain through his shoulders and down the middle of his back.

A foul, sewer-like odor oozes from the creature. Brock retches. Thrashing and rolling on the ground he pushes hard against the supernatural being but is too weak and no match for it.

"Help me, Jesus!" he cries out in desperation.

A burst of radiant energy suddenly illuminates the train yard.

The demon releases Brock and crouches low, shielding its eyes from the light. "Have you come to torture me, Son of God?" The demon utters a low sound.

"Be still," a powerful voice reproves the evil spirit sharply.

Stunned, Brock rolls over on his belly and lifts his head to look for the source of light and the voice.

A giant sphere shines through a door like the opening of the black night sky. Myriads of gold and white glisten from the lustrous beam. Brock is transfixed by what he sees. His strength returns, and he slowly rises to his feet.

"Use your sword!" the heavenly voice commands.

Sword?

"Say My words."

It is as if the voice had read his mind. Brock tries to remember something about putting on the armor of God to stand against the devil's tricks. *Yes, that's it. The sword of the Spirit is the Word of God* [Ephesians 6:13-17].

He searches for a verse to battle this ruler of darkness. And then he finds one he learned as a kid when he went to church with Aunt Millie.

He turns to face the evil spirit. "For God so loved the world that he gave his only begotten Son that whosoever believeth in Him shall not perish but have everlasting life."

A brilliant, jagged bolt of electricity flashes from one end of the sky to the other followed by thousands of crashing and booming sounds. The railroad cars shake and rattle.

The demon's clawed hand covers its ears as it collapses to the ground, screaming.

"In the name of Jesus," Brock says with authority, "be gone!"

The demon lets out a screech before he disintegrates, leaving the sewer stench to linger. Then as quickly as it came the thundering noise stops.

Brock slowly turns around and looks up into the glorious light.

"Lord?"

"I am the Alpha and the Omega, the first and the last, the beginning and the end."

Brock feels an intense trance-like joy and drops face down on the ground.

The heavenly voice continues. "Your faith has been tried and tested in the fiery furnace of affliction. Rejoice! Very soon you will be praised and honored at My appearing."

The iridescent golden light beam moves and merges with Brock's body. An avalanche of love pours through him. It is a love beyond his wildest imagination; it is the love of a father he never knew; it is the love of a man giving his life for his friend; it is the love of forgiveness for all the bad things he had ever done. Brock absorbs and basks in His glory and love.

"Brock," the Lord says, "I have spared your life because one of My sheep is lost. I have chosen you to go and find her and bring her to Me."

Brock lifts his head and stares into the light. "Why me, Lord? I am not worthy. Why not choose Jesse or somebody else?"

"Because it is My will as it was with My servants before you."

Brock's thoughts go to His servant Moses whom God chose to lead the children of Israel out of Egypt. Moses didn't think he was worthy because he was a lousy speaker with a speech impediment.

And then there was Jonah whom God chose to warn the people of Nineveh to repent or their city would be destroyed. Jonah tried to ignore God by sailing away; but a storm arose, and Jonah fell into the sea and was swallowed up by a big fish.

"Yes, Lord," Brock answers earnestly. "I am Your servant. Your will be done."

The door in the sky closes, and black swallows up the beautiful beam of light, leaving Brock in darkness.

"Wait, Lord. . .where do I go? Where do I find Your lost sheep?"

"Follow the iron snake to where the bear flows with gold."

Who shall separate us from the love of Christ? shall tribulation, or distress, or persecution, or famine, or nakedness, or peril, or sword? As it is written, For thy sake we are killed all the day long; we are accounted as sheep for the slaughter. Nay, in all these things we are more than conquerors through him that loved us. For I am persuaded, that neither death, nor life, nor angels, nor principalities, nor powers, nor things present, nor things to come, nor height, nor depth, nor any other creature, shall be able to separate us from the love of God, which is in Christ Jesus our Lord.
Romans 8:35-39

CHAPTER

14

"I think that one's still alive," says an unfamiliar voice.

Desperately Brock attempts to open his eyes, but they feel as if they are glued shut. Unable to move, he feels a hand touch his throat then press against his carotid artery.

"He's alive all right—David! Bring the tarp over here."

Brock feels his body lifted off the ground just before he falls back into unconsciousness.

****

A wet cloth presses against Brock's forehead stirring him awake. A trickle of water glides down his swollen cheek as blood pounds in his temples.

Forcing his eyes open, a blurred shadow hovers over him.

A soft hand with long fingers lifts his arm.

Blinking rapidly, his vision begins to clear. His eyes fix on a lovely young woman with black hair pulled back into a braid; her bangs skim her eyebrows and compliment her heart-shaped face.

The woman's brown eyes, almost fiery, catch Brock staring at her. Her mouth turns up at the corners, and she glances away.

Who is she? Brock asks himself. *She looks so familiar.*

The burning sensation under his armpit forces him back to reality. Inwardly he groans, and his teeth clench as the young woman tends to his wounds.

Carefully she places his arm down next to his side on top of the sheet.

Clothed in white shorts and a blue cotton T-shirt, the young woman walks across the room to a metal filing cabinet and pulls down a cardboard box.

"Oh, good! You're awake!" a jovial voice booms from the other side of the room.

Brock turns his head slightly and finds a middle-aged man in blue jeans and an army-green T-shirt walking toward him with a cup in his hand. His jaw is covered with a short, gray beard.

"Here." The man smiles. "Drink up."

Excruciating pain shoots throughout his body when he tries to move. He manages to push himself up to his elbows and take the cup. He presses it against his cracked lips, sips then asks, "What is it?"

"Willow bark!"

"Willow bark? Isn't that like aspirin?"

"Yes, it sure is! It'll bring your fever down and help ease your pain."

Brock presses the cup back to his lips and drinks the warm, red liquid till it's gone.

"Thank you." He passes the empty cup back to the pepper-haired man then wipes his mouth with his hand. Glancing about the small room Brock notices a desk, a bookcase and a filing cabinet. "Where am I?"

"In an office of a vacant warehouse next to the train station."

"Oh." Brock does recall passing a number of loading docks and a train station as he, Jesse and Arturo fled from town. This must be one of the buildings.

"Who are you?"

"Well, Brock." The man chuckles out loud. "I'm nobody."

"Nobody?" Brock tries to ignore the aching pain pulsating through his forehead.

"I'm nobody without Jesus! But my friends call me Buddy." The man grins from ear to ear. "And that beautiful young lady over there is Nicole!" He winks.

Brock shoots a glance at Nicole then turns back to Buddy.

"How did you know my name?"

"I recognized you from the WNN (World News Network). And your trial, that was big news. . . ."

Nicole returns to Brock's side with a jar in one hand and a paint brush in the other. She sticks the brush into the jar of dark amber goo then lifts his arm and paints the sticky substance onto his skin.

Wincing occasionally, Brock tries hard to conceal his agony from Nicole. He thinks she looks familiar but can't quite remember where he's seen her before. . . . Then he remembers—*Earth angel!* The girl he saw on the street corner where the prophet was speaking—she was with the kid that had the tattoos on his arm.

"What's that?" Brock nods at the jar.

"It's honey!" Buddy answers.

"Honey?"

"Yes, honey is a great antibacterial for wounds. It's kind of like hydrogen peroxide."

Brock knew what honey was used for; he'd read it in his survivor books. He just didn't know the goop she was painting on him was honey.

Nicole lowers his arm to the bed sheet then paints a small piece of white cotton with honey and presses it against his forehead like a sticker.

Finished, she takes the items and places them back in the box on top of the filing cabinet then walks to the door.

"Thank you, Nicole!" Brock strains to smile.

She doesn't respond.

Buddy hurries over and pulls the door handle. "I will see you at the house." He speaks very loud.

She nods, and Buddy closes the door after her.

More questions form in Brock's mind. "What happened? Where's Jesse? Is he all right?"

Buddy hesitates. "David saw you at the tracks with the American Union police. He came and got me after they left. We found you were still alive so we brought you back here." He grabs a blood-soaked turquoise shirt from the back of the black leather chair behind a desk.

Brock recognizes his polo shirt.

"It's a miracle you're alive, son. Here, let me show you."

Buddy steps toward Brock. "Look, there's a bullet hole here." His finger pokes through a hole over the breast pocket. "You were hit, but the bullet didn't pass through. It stopped in your pocket—and look, there's even some shrapnel inside!" Buddy's fingers disappear inside the pocket then reappear grasping tiny metal fragments.

Brock's jaw drops open. He remembers being shot. It felt like a bullet blasted his heart. But how did the bullet stop and not pass through his shirt? It surely had to be the hand of God. It truly was a miracle.

"Another bullet grazed your underarm, but it's nothing serious. We just have to keep an eye on it for infection."

The office door opens, and in walks a dark-headed boy with a paper sack in his hand. Brock recognizes him as the kid who was with Nicole.

"Set it over there, David." Buddy points to the desk.

The boy looks at Brock with big, brown eyes.

"What happened to Jesse?" Brock asks again, deep concern in his voice.

"Jesse?" Buddy's eyebrow arches. "Is Jesse the man who was with you?"

"Yes."

"I'm sorry." Buddy's voice quiets. "He didn't make it. But we were able to give him a proper burial."

Brock's heart twists at the news. *I've lost my friend.* He pictures his cellmate's smiling face and twinkling gray eyes. His chest tightens, and a tear rolls down his cheek. *Jesse is with the Lord now—where he wanted to be. I sure will miss him, but at least he got a proper burial.* He had heard that in some places the World Union impaled the bodies or heads of dead Christians and Jews on posts along major highways to send fear to those who resisted the New World Order. If anyone deserved a proper burial it was Jesse.

"Well, I think that's it for now—oh, wait!" Buddy steps over and grabs the paper bag from the desk. He peeks inside then looks up. "If you get hungry here are a couple of hard-boiled eggs and some fruit and water. And there's a solar flashlight on the chair next to your cot." He sets the brown paper bag on the metal folding chair.

"Also David found a duffle bag in the shed—he thought it might be yours. It's over there." Buddy leans his head toward the opposite corner of the office.

"Oh, I almost forgot—if you need to relieve yourself, there's a bucket at the foot of your cot."

Brock's gaze shifts to a round orange bucket lined with white plastic.

"Thanks."

Buddy walks across the room and opens the door, with David at his heels. "I'll check on you first thing in the morning after curfew."

The door closes behind them.

Brock scoots down on the cot and arranges the pillow behind his head. He tries to dismiss the throbbing under his arm and closes his eyes. The willow bark tea is beginning to kick in and relax him.

He thanks God for saving his life and for being rescued by fellow believers. He wishes he could have saved Jesse's life. A picture of Jesse in his starring role in *Zen Warrior* comes to mind, and then he reflects on how tragic it was that Jesse got involved in drugs like so many other movie stars. But God heard his prayer and miraculously delivered him from his addiction. Brock feels blessed to have known Jesse even though it was for such a short time.

His thoughts drift back to the earthquake and how he escaped the prison fire; if it wasn't for that guard letting them out they would have all burned to death. Then he recalls aloud the strange riddle the guard spoke: "Four of you will be tried by fire; three will not burn. Of the three, two will fall and one will be spared." He repeats to himself: "*Of the three, two will fall and one will be spared.*"

It starts to make sense to him now. "'Two will fall'— that was Jesse and Cornelius—they both fell, and I was the one who was spared."

He repeats the rest of the riddle: "'Woe to the fourth one who will be scorched by the fiery furnace where there is weeping and gnashing of teeth." Arturo was the fourth one.

That the trial of your faith, being much more precious than of gold that perisheth, though it be tried with fire, might be found unto praise and honour and glory at the appearing of Jesus Christ.
1 Peter 1:7

CHAPTER
15

Three quick taps sound on the door before it swings open.

"Good morning!"

Brock lifts his head and turns his eyes toward the door. It is Buddy.

"Morning," Brock replies. He scoots up and tucks the pillow behind his back.

Buddy closes the door then steps into the room. "How's our guest of honor feeling today?"

"Guest of honor?"

"Yes! It's not every day you meet someone who has survived the firing squad of Satan's regime!"

"True." Brock shudders. "Feeling much better today, thanks."

Buddy crosses to Brock and studies his face. "It looks like the swelling is coming down, and the black and blue bruises around your eyes are starting to fade."

Buddy bends over and picks up the flashlight from the chair then walks over to the window and places it on the window ledge between the blinds. As he turns back he says, "I hope you're hungry. Nicole will be up shortly with some breakfast."

"Yeah."

Seeing Nicole again makes Brock smile inside.

Buddy drops down in the office chair and props his feet on the desk. After about five minutes of silence in the room, Nicole shows up. She walks over and hands a plate of food to Brock.

"Thank you!" Brock smiles and tries to catch her eye, but she turns and walks back to the door.

"Thank you, Nicole!" Buddy says.

Nicole doesn't acknowledge him as she closes the door.

Bummed that Nicole left, Brock scarfs down the fluffy yellow scrambled eggs sprinkled with salt.

"Very delicious." He sets the empty plate on the metal chair next to his cot.

Buddy stands. "Can I get you anything before I leave? A book? A Bible?"

Brock's eyebrows rise. "You have a Bible?"

"Sure do!"

The idea of getting his hands on a Bible again excites Brock. He can't remember how many times he'd wished he had one. Before he was arrested Bibles were outlawed and replaced with Peter Roma's "New Gospel." To be found with a Bible was punishable by death. The media created a big event and promoted Bible-burning parties. He had reported from one of these parties at Santa Monica Beach. The sand glowed bright crimson and orange as people joyously sang around a ten-foot-high stack of burning Bibles.

"Yes, I'd love to have a Bible."

"I think I may have one in here." Buddy pulls open a desk drawer, lifts out a folded paper then shuts the drawer.

"I thought I had one here, but I guess not. Here's a newspaper if you want till I find you one."

"Thanks."

Buddy leaves the room.

Eager to find out what's been happening in the world since he was arrested, Brock opens the neatly folded publication and scans the news articles, features, reviews and advertisements. The main headline of *The North American Times* catches his attention: "MAN CAUGHT HOARDING FOOD ARRESTED."

He skims the next headline: "SWEEPING SEARCH FINDS NO TRACE OF MISSING PACIFIC UNION AIRLINER." The next headline stops him: "130 PEOPLE PUBLICLY BEHEADED ACROSS CALIFORNIA, INCLUDING A SIXTEEN-YEAR-OLD GIRL."

Becky? His heart flutters as an image of Becky Silver comes to his mind. Holding his breath, he reads on.

"The World Union publicly executed as many as 130 people on Solday (Friday), including a sixteen-year-old girl—some for infractions as minor as stealing dog food. Many of the victims were convicted of rape, murder, armed robbery and drug trafficking, all of which are punishable by death under the World Union Constitution. Most of the victims were charged with possessing a Bible, Aquarian News reported."

Brock is relieved when he doesn't see Becky's name. He prays they released her into her mother's care.

His gaze shifts to the next headline: "GROUP CLAIMING TO BE ISRAEL'S SANHEDRIN ACCEPTS MAITREYAS AS THE MESSIAH."

"Jerusalem. —Jewish rabbi Eli Abrahamson, who claims to be the leading justice of the Sanhedrin (the supreme council and court of justice among the Jews), has named Lord Maitreyas the Prince of Peace thus fulfilling messianic prophecy.

"'Peace has come to the whole world through Lord Maitreyas,' said Rabbi Abrahamson at a news conference recently. 'He has broken the bow and sword and has abolished them from Israel!' The rabbi quoted several scriptures from the Torah, including Micah 4:3: 'And he shall judge among many people, and rebuke strong nations afar off; and they shall beat their swords into plowshares, and their spears into pruning hooks: nation shall not lift up a sword against nation, neither shall they learn war anymore.'

"World Union police have arrested at least 140 Jewish men at the Wailing Wall who protested in opposition over the rabbi's recent remarks.

"Security is strict at Mount Moriah as prayer and animal sacrifices continue at the ancient tabernacle of Moses which has been erected for worship during the rebuilding of the third holy temple. The tent sanctuary was recently discovered in Jeremiah's Cave along with the Ark of the Covenant and the incense altar."

Brock reflects on the article. *Even the Jewish rabbi has been deceived into believing Maitreyas is the Messiah. Jesus is the one who will fulfill the prophecy not Maitreyas. And the animal sacrifices—it's happening just as the Bible prophesied.*

The next headline jumps out at him: "BROCK SUMMERS ACCEPTS LORD MAITREYAS AFTER AN EMOTIONAL BREAKDOWN. By Bob Brown, North American Union Reporter."

Slapped by a whirlwind of apprehension he reads on.

"Solday afternoon trial resumed in the case of the People of the World Union vs. Brock Lee Summers. Story continues on page 7."

Brock flips to page 7 and locates the story.

"Defending himself, Summers, dressed in an orange prison jumpsuit, struggled at times to maintain his composure on the witness stand. The famous reporter broke down in tears after the prosecutor was able to show that the World Union had enough evidence to convict him for crimes against the government which were punishable by death.

"Summers was tried on five counts including blasphemy against the World Union and providing material support for terrorism after the confiscation of his computer, credit card receipts and newspaper.

"Summers tearfully accepted Judge William Davis's pardon by renouncing his faith.

"Before being arrested, Summers was a journalist for WNN News and covered late-breaking stories as well as in-depth investigative reports. His celebrity status had riveted worldwide attention.

"In a special interview Summers expressed his joy over his decision and said he was looking forward to serving Lord Maitreyas and becoming a world citizen."

Brock slams the paper down on the floor. His brows pull together, and his eyes stare straight ahead.

He hears a rapping sound, and the door swings open.

Still seething, Brock looks up to see Buddy.

"Here's your Bible!"

"Thanks." Brock's voice is disgruntled, and a frown is still on his forehead.

"What's the matter?"

"I can't believe they printed such lies about me in the paper."

Buddy sets the Bible on the desk. "What do you mean?"

"That idiot Bob what's-his-name said I was looking forward to serving Lord Maitreyas. That's a bald-faced lie—I said no such thing."

"Well, you know how biased and controlled the media is."

"Yeah, that's for sure. If anyone knows this I do. I can't begin to tell you how many times my editors rewrote my stories. That's one of the reasons I started my own paper, to tell the truth."

"So, Brock, what is the truth?"

The frown on Brock's forehead dissipates. "Oh, yeah,

sure, you have a right to know."

Buddy rolls the office chair next to Brock's cot and eases himself down.

"Well, the part about me in court was true; I did agree to renounce my faith. I was ordered to go to the courtyard and kneel to a Maitreyas statue, but for some reason the bailiff stuck me in a small room and forgot about me.

"The next thing I know. . . ." Brock tells Buddy how he witnessed the executions then was sent back to prison and Jesse was his cellmate; about the earthquake and how they escaped from the fire with the help of a guard who spoke a strange riddle; about the prophet in town who pointed to him and said God had chosen him; how Jesse helped him pray and repent for denying Jesus in court; how they escaped the police the first time and hid in the shed till they were discovered the next morning; how they were told to deny their faith or be shot and how Arturo complied; about the dream he had after he was shot, that Jesus told him to go find His lost sheep and he was sure it had something to do with the part of the riddle.

"We figured out what the iron snake was, but I'm still not clear on what 'the bear flows with gold' means."

"What's the iron snake?" Buddy asks.

"It's the railroad tracks. Arturo figured it out."

"Oh, so that's why you guys were on the tracks."

"Yes. The plan was to follow them and see where we ended up."

Buddy stares at the floor for a few moments then looks up at Brock.

"You're to follow the railroad tracks to the Bear River—the river that flows with gold!"

"What?"

"The Bear River—it flows with gold! It was famous during the California Gold Rush!"

Brock mouths the riddle slowly. "Follow the railroad tracks to the bear that flows with gold—the Bear River! Yes, that has to be it!"

CHAPTER
16

Handling the leather bound book with great care, Brock brushes the dust off the cover unveiling the words HOLY BIBLE embellished in gold letters. He thumbs through the crisp clean pages with no visible sign of wear.

"It's yours if you want," Buddy says. "I have plenty more where that came from."

"Thanks!" Brock's attention is focused on the sacred texts. "So where'd you get it?"

"It's kind of a long story."

Brock closes the book thoughtfully and holds it against his chest. "I'd like to hear it."

"Sure, why not."

Buddy sits back down in the office chair next to Brock. He leans forward, resting his elbows on his knees.

With a somber look on his face he says, "I wasn't always a believer. I did some terrible things I'm deeply ashamed of." He pauses for a minute then says, "I was like Saul. I used to persecute and execute Jews and Christians."

Brock's eyebrows shoot up. "You executed Jews and Christians?"

"Yes, but, thank goodness, I found the Lord Jesus, and He has forgiven me. Now I've made it my mission to help them."

"Wow! So what happened?"

"I was in the military—and, uh, technically I still am in

the military—but that's a whole 'nother story.

"Anyway, when the Bible ban went into effect we confiscated hundreds of thousands of Bibles. We destroyed most of them but kept some to plant on our enemies, whether they were Christians or not."

Brock thinks back to one of his co-workers who was arrested and jailed for having a Bible. He found it puzzling at the time because this man never appeared to be a Christian. He wonders now if he was framed.

"So when did you become a Christian?"

Buddy leans back in the chair. "Okay, I'll start from the beginning. You see, I was born and raised by Luciferians—"

"Luciferians?"

"If the subject bothers you I can stop."

"Oh, no, sorry. You just caught me off guard. Go on."

"When I was a kid my parents dedicated me to Lucifer in a secret ceremony. I was schooled and taught the rites and rituals of the Secret Order of the Illumined Men. I was taught to hate Christians and Jews and told they were our enemies. Lucifer was my god, and the world was my footstool as long as I kept his ways."

"Were you abused as a child? I heard terrible stories of children who were used in satanic rituals."

"No, I was never abused. If you're born with the sacred bloodline you're not ritually abused."

Buddy continues. "On my eighteenth birthday I was initiated as a high priest and ordered to join the U.S. military to recruit personnel into the occult. I set up several covens and was also involved in ordering and setting up the guillotines at the military bases and re-education centers.

"Fast forward twenty years—I had a dream. In this dream I was the high priest of my coven so I sent some people to harass a preacher. They came back to me terrified and said they could not get inside the preacher's house. Frustrated, I decided to go myself. When I got there, standing at the front door was a giant faceless being wearing a white robe. I tried to push past it but couldn't. The being's face illuminated and became clear. He had a sad look in his eyes. 'Why do you persecute God's children?' he asked me. 'You need Jesus.'

"I woke up then, and I remember wondering how come I couldn't push past this angelic being when I knew Satan was more powerful. I shrugged it off as only a dream.

"Then about a week later I was driving home from work with my windows rolled down. The car in front of me stopped for a red light so I slowed to a stop also. I noticed one of these long-haired, crazy guys on the street corner yelling, 'REPENT! THE END IS NEAR!' The guy suddenly looked in my direction and ran toward my car. I wanted to drive forward but couldn't because of the car in front of me. The guy leaned through my window and said, 'Why do you persecute God's children? You need Jesus.'

"I sat there stunned. I remember thinking it was the same exact message the angel had said in my dream. The driver in the car behind me blasted his horn, bringing me to my senses. I looked around, and the guy was gone.

"I pondered this for a few days. Then Linda, who was one of the witches in my coven, said something to me as we passed in the hall at work—'You need Jesus'—and walked away.

"Now why would she say that? I asked myself. Jesus was our sworn enemy, and we risked death if we left the coven. I noticed something was different about Linda though. I couldn't quite pin it down.

"Then there was the nuclear bomb attack in Charleston."

Brock recalls news coverage on the attack in

Charleston, South Carolina. They blamed it on terrorists. He had always wondered why they picked Charleston of all places.

Water collects in Buddy's eyes. "That's when I lost my wife and son."

Buddy is quiet for a moment.

"It nearly destroyed me. I was angry because I wasn't informed of the date so I could evacuate my family. It was a government-staged, false flag attack—a secret act committed by one group pretending to be a targeted enemy while attacking their own forces or people—and I knew it was either going to be in San Diego or Charleston. Had I been informed I could have saved my family. The high priest in the Order of the Illumined Men said my wife and son were sacrificed to Lucifer and that I should be honored. I know this sounds heartless, but at the time I didn't care if I sacrificed other people's families—but not mine.

"I was so angry. I got ahold of one of the Christian Bibles and began reading it out of rebellion, I guess. It was a King James Bible, not one of the distorted New Age types. I opened it to Acts 9 and began reading. Words can't describe my feelings when I read the part about Jesus meeting Saul on the road to Damascus and saying, 'Saul, Saul, why do you persecute Me?' I felt as if Jesus was speaking to me through the pages. I remember I nearly dropped the Bible on the floor.

"I was troubled and couldn't talk to anyone about it. I finally decided to meet with Linda, the witch who'd mentioned Jesus to me in the hallway. She confessed to me that she was no longer a witch but a Christian and that the Lord spoke to her in a dream to share Jesus with me. She shared her testimony about how she became saved and said she would pray for me. I remember I liked the idea that Jesus gave Himself as a sacrifice unlike Lucifer who demanded a human sacrifice.

"The death of my son continued to plague me. I had bad dreams and nightmares. I came to a point where I didn't care anymore about anything. I was suicidal.

"One day I cried out that if Jesus was who Linda said He was I wanted Him to show me a sign.

"A few days later I stopped in at one of the W.U. facilities in Valencia, just outside of Los Angeles. I was walking down the hall when I saw a young boy sitting in a chair next to his father whose hands were handcuffed. My heart nearly stopped in my chest; the boy looked just like my son Justin.

"I wondered how my son could be sitting there with this strange man when he was dead. Maybe they made a mistake. Maybe he didn't die in Charleston. I nearly wept right there in the hallway. I called out Justin's name. The boy looked up at me, but he had such fear in his eyes that I realized it wasn't him."

Buddy pauses to catch his breath.

"I couldn't get over how much he looked like Justin— he was a spitting image of him.

"I inquired about the man and the boy. I was told the father was Jewish and was going to be sent to a camp to be exterminated. Since the boy was only half Jewish he would be sent to Camp Pendleton for medical experimentation.

"Although I was raised to hate Jews, I could not bring myself to hate this young boy. I made a pact right then and there with God that if I could somehow save this child and raise him as my own it was the sign I had prayed for and I would accept Jesus as my Savior. Because of my high rank and connections, I was able to rescue the boy by telling them my intentions of raising him as my own and training him in the ways of the occult, that our coven would use him as bait to lure others."

Brock remembers David.

"Is David the boy you rescued?"

"Yes!" Buddy beams. "That's him! Isn't it ironic that God gave me a Jewish boy to love as my own?"

Brock recalls when he was arrested in Southern California and held in a box car with Becky Silver; she had mentioned she was half Jewish and from Valencia and that her father and brother David were taken by government officials in the middle of the night.

"Do you know the boy's last name?"

"Yes, it's Silver, David Silver. . . ."

CHAPTER

17

"Good morning!" Buddy smiles as he enters the room.

Brock sits up in his bed and notices the brown paper bag in Buddy's hand.

"Where's David? Isn't he coming?"

Buddy walks over and sets the bag on the desk and rolls out the chair.

"No. He left yesterday with some members to deliver supplies to believers in Sacramento. We figured the authorities would be busy with the earthquake so we decided to take advantage of the situation and get much-needed supplies out."

Brock is disappointed. "I was hoping to talk to him and tell him I met his sister, Becky. When will he be back?"

"It's hard to say. If things go well, in about four or five days."

****

Standing in front of the window Brock peeks through the mini-blinds. The morning sun glistens on the railroad tracks below. Brock yearns to get out into the fresh air again. He has been cooped up in this small room and is restless. Last night he'd read the Bible until the solar batteries finally died, and this morning he investigated the building where he found a small kitchen, more offices and many locked doors.

He hears a tap on the door, and Buddy enters. "Good morning!"

Brock turns from the window. "Morning!" He realizes David still hasn't returned when he sees Buddy holding a brown paper bag.

Buddy closes the door, walks over and sets the bag on the desk then pulls out the chair and sits down.

Brock plops down on the army cot. This has been their daily routine. Buddy comes in the morning, and the men chat until Nicole shows up with breakfast, and then she changes his bandages. In the evening, before curfew, Buddy comes back with his dinner and then leaves.

"How are you feeling today?"

"Great!" Brock scratches the back of his head. "I think I'm gonna head out in the morning."

"So soon?" Buddy leans back in the chair and throws his feet onto the desk. He crosses his arms over his chest.

"Yeah."

"You know you're welcome to stay here if you want. We could sure use you in RAD."

Buddy had told Brock about their group called RAD in one of their earlier conversations: Resisters Against Darkness. They recruit and help other believers and work together finding and bartering food and supplies.

After Buddy's conversion he had secretly diverted shipments of food, medical supplies, military clothing, boots, blankets and cots from underground storage facilities the military had been stockpiling. He'd hidden them in various locations along the railways, including the building they were in.

"It's tempting, but I'm gonna head out to Bear River."

"I understand."

"I'm thinking I'll leave tomorrow, early before the sun

comes up. How far do you think it is to the river?"

Buddy's forehead wrinkles. "I'd say about fifteen miles."

"So I just follow the tracks outside till I hit the river?"

Buddy shakes his head. "Don't follow those tracks. They dead-end past the boxcar storage yard. You'll need to go back to the center of town; there you'll see the train bridge. Cross the river then follow the tracks north until they split then follow the tracks right, and then you'll come upon the town of Rayburn. Go past Rayburn a couple of miles then head north through the hills. You should run into Bear River."

"Sounds simple enough."

****

Buddy props a backpack against the wall. "I scrounged up some food and supplies for you to take with you to the river."

Brock scoots up in the cot and leans back against the pillow. He eyes the camouflage pack; a black chest strap and waist belt dangle to the floor.

"Nice, thanks!"

Buddy heads to the office chair. "Nicole will be up in a sec."

Nicole? Brock's eyebrows arch. *What's she coming for? Buddy always came in the evening alone.*

Brock's legs swing off the cot. He hurries over to the duffle bag and pulls out a T-shirt and slips it over his head then runs his fingers through his hair. He retreats to the cot and sits with his back against the wall and his arms crossed over his chest.

"I wasn't expecting Nicole."

"Since it's your last night we thought it would be nice

for you to have a special meal. I hope you like beef stroganoff?"

"Yes, but she doesn't have to go to all that trouble."

Buddy laughs. "It's no trouble. It's an MRE."

"Oh, an MRE!" [Meals Ready to Eat]. He had several packets stuffed in his bug-out back at home.

"I have pallets of them stored away in the basement, and I pull them out in emergencies or special occasions like this one." He grins then shuts his eyes.

The door pushes open, and Nicole passes through carrying a steaming bowl wrapped in a towel. Brock didn't even notice the food but gawked at how pretty she looked in a hot pink sundress. Her beauty mesmerizes him.

White sandals click across the wood floor.

"Thank you, Nicole!" Brock smiles as he takes the bowl from her hands. "You sure do look nice in your dress!"

Meeting his eyes, Nicole smiles politely then turns and walks to the metal filing cabinet.

Brock stares at her thick lovely hair that hangs loose on her bare shoulders. It's the first time he's seen her wear it down. She's always worn it in a single braid down the middle of her back.

He twirls the fork buried in the egg noodles then takes a bite. He swallows then stabs the beef, mushrooms and onions, devouring them. As he enjoys his meal he watches Nicole rummage through the box pulling out honey, gauze and other items and setting them on the floor.

Brock glances over at Buddy whose legs are propped on the desk; his eyes are closed, and he snores softly.

Grabbing the items, Nicole walks over and nudges Buddy awake.

Startled, Buddy's eyes fling open, and he drops his legs to the floor. He stands and takes the items out of Nicole's hand and places them on the desk. "Brock, here's the honey and some bandages for you to use till your wounds heal."

"Thanks!" Brock sets the empty bowl down on the chair next to him.

Looking at Nicole Buddy says, "I guess it's time to say good-bye to Brock."

Brock leaps to his feet. He hates saying good-bye. Although he is anxious to head out to his new adventure he feels a sense of sadness.

"See you around." He smiles and looks down at Nicole whose head comes to his shoulder.

Nicole looks up, and for a second their eyes lock, and he stares deep into her soul. Her mouth turns up at the corners, and then quickly she looks down and sweeps the floor with her gaze. She reaches up and tugs at a brown leather cord tied around her neck then pulls it over her head.

Brock feels her soft fingers grab his hand and gently place something cold and hard inside.

In a swift movement her hands move to his shoulders, and she plants a kiss on his left cheek then turns and walks away.

Brock's heart nearly stops as he watches her disappear through the door.

Standing with his mouth gaping open he utters softly, "And I thought she didn't like me!"

"What do you mean?"

"Whenever I tried to talk to her she just ignored me."

"Oh." Buddy laughs. "You didn't know?"

"Know what?"

"Nicole is deaf."

"Deaf?" Brock is stunned by Buddy's announcement. "Really. She's deaf?" It was more of a statement than a question. That explained it. He never once suspected she couldn't hear him. He just thought she was shy or didn't like him or maybe even had a boyfriend or something.

"I thought I was striking out with her." He laughs.

"In fact, I think she likes you an awful lot."

"Why do you say that?"

"Because she gave you her most prized possession."

Brock opens his hand slowly and glances down to see a stainless steel cross.

"This?"

"Yes. When we found Nicole, she was badly beaten and naked. We carried her to safety when we realized she had something in her hand; it was that cross."

Brock squeezes the metal between his fingers as he pictures Nicole.

"I can't even imagine how terrible that must have been for her."

"We don't know her story because she can't speak. David really bonded with her and sticks to her like glue."

Brock is overcome with emotion. How she must have suffered. Poor, sweet Nicole. He wished he had known she was deaf.

He thinks back to the first time he saw her and how captivated she seemed to be with the prophet. He was sure she could hear him as she smiled and nodded at the prophet's words.

"Can she hear prophets?"

"I don't know about prophets, but some of our members say she can hear angels. In one of our meetings we were singing when she looked up and suddenly her face lit up and she began clapping and dancing."

A pleasant feeling envelops Brock. He caresses the pendant then slips the cord over his head and tucks it under his shirt where it rests against his heart.

Patting his chest he says, "I will treasure this always."

CHAPTER

18

All is quiet except the sound of tree branches swaying in the warm breeze coming down from the mountains and the babbling sound of water cascading over steep rocks.

"Okay, Lord," Brock mumbles under his breath. "I'm here. Where is your lost sheep?"

Exhausted, he slips off the backpack and props it against the straight thick trunk of a towering Ponderosa pine. Sweat pools under the arms of his army-green T-shirt. The muscles in his back and shoulders are inflamed by the heavy load. His mouth is dry and his throat parched.

The roar of the river grows louder, and the temperature drops as he makes his way to the water's edge.

Gravel punctures his knees when he kneels down and thrusts his cupped hands into the whirling current. He scoops the liquid and gulps it down as if he hasn't had a drop of water in months.

Humming gnats collect around his eyes. With a grunt, Brock plops down on his hind quarters. Grimacing, he kicks off his shoes then peels off the dingy, sticky socks soaked in red around the ankles.

He pulls a black leather sheath out of the right pocket of his camouflage shorts and slides the cover back. After admiring the sharp, stainless steel blade Buddy gave him he slips the knife back into its case and tosses it on the ground next to his shoes.

Wading into the river he is careful not to slip on the slick, moss-covered rocks. Chill bumps break out on his arms as he lowers himself into the water, soaking his shorts and T-shirt. He sits down on a submerged rock and splashes water on his face and trunk, scrubbing hard to remove the dirt and grime before dipping his head under, sending a cold chill up his spine.

The current tugs at him, trying to pull him downstream. Soon his body relaxes and begins to adapt to the cool temperature.

His eyes are heavy from lack of sleep and thin air. Yesterday he walked along the railroad tracks in the sweltering temperature when he'd run out of water. His body wanted to stop and rest, but he ignored it and pushed hard walking all through the night, hoping he would reach the Bear River in the morning.

Small fish dart between the rocks, and a dragonfly beats its wings wildly. He thinks of the tiny robotic dragonfly drones used by the military to spy and track resisters. Although it feels safe here in God's country, he must stay alert at all times.

Water drips as he stands to his feet. Slowly he makes his way over to shore and puts on his socks and shoes then slips the knife back inside his shorts.

Feeling refreshed, he retrieves his backpack and continues up the river.

Scattered along the way are remnants of trash, a soda can and a shredded towel caught in the branches of a bush.

Up ahead, a barrier of rocks obstructs the water flow.
A dam.

Something hard strikes him in the left shoulder.

Surprised, he looks around.

A scraggly, gray-haired woman stands on the river

bank, her face engraved with deep lines. Deranged gibberish flows from her lips as she bends over to pick up another rock.

"GO AWAY!" she yells, her words clear.

Shielding his face with his arms, Brock ducks as a rock hurls past him.

"GO AWAY! NO TRESPASSING!" The old woman hunts the ground with her eyes.

"Okay, lady, okay. I'm just passing through."

What a nut! He rubs his shoulder.

Brock continues up the steep terrain through the rugged canyon. The snow-fed river twists and rumbles over ledges as it carves out its gorges deep and wide. Water dashes against great boulders.

Brock reflects on the crazy old woman and wonders if maybe she's the one God sent him to find. With that in mind he decides to look for a place to make camp; he's hungry and hasn't eaten anything since last night. He'll figure out a way to approach the old woman later.

A flash of blue catches his attention up ahead.

A spurt of adrenaline releases through his body, and he quickly drops to the ground and lies motionless on his belly hoping nobody saw him.

After a few minutes he inches forward for a better look. He discovers the blue thing is a tarp made into a canopy that covers a black chest of drawers and several boxes.

Wary, he waits and listens but hears nothing unusual.

Rising to his knees, he drops the backpack to the ground then pulls out his knife.

Squatting on his haunches he crawls toward the camp, keeping his eyes steady and intent.

A small pink bicycle lies beside a gray-and-blue, two-man dome tent. Two vintage green-and-white webbed, folding lounge chairs are propped in front of a fire pit filled with ashes. He notices a strange white powdery substance sprinkled all around the perimeter of the camp and over the tent.

I wonder what the white stuff is for.

Holding his knife to his side, he stands and steps cautiously into the campsite. His nose wrinkles from the stench of rotting garbage.

"Hello? Hello? Is anybody there?"

No answer.

Flies swarm over two plastic trash barrels overflowing with garbage and spilling onto the ground. A burned-out candle sits on a crude piece of plywood used for a table. Trails of ants cross the wood and into empty cans of food. A blue two-piece bathing suit and a black pair of men's swim shorts are draped over a rope tied between two pine trees.

The camp seems empty. He releases a deep sigh.

A fishing rod on the ground catches his eye. *Sure could use that.*

He opens a white ice chest and finds it empty. Puzzled, he wonders if the occupants have abandoned the camp. It just doesn't make sense, though, because they left everything behind.

He decides to come back tomorrow to see if anyone has returned. He's hoping they're friendly so he can barter with them for the use of their fishing pole.

He pulls an empty two-liter soda bottle from the trash barrel then retrieves his backpack.

The Bear River jostles over friendly rapids and meanders down the canyon. Up ahead it bends right, and giant boulders are strewn on both sides of the riverbank. Leaving his shoes on, Brock crosses the channel and stands below the giant gray rock and looks around.

This might be a good spot. It has a full view of the river up and down the canyon, and I'll be well hidden behind the rocks.

The backpack weighs him down as he climbs up the gentle slope. He tosses the soda bottle on the ground then drops the backpack beside it and collapses on the dirt. He lays his head on the lumpy pack and closes his eyes. The soothing sound of the water plunging over the falls relaxes him. . . .

****

Brock swallows the last few bites of teriyaki with rice right out of the MRE pouch as he sits next to the fire. He's upset with himself for falling asleep. He'd planned on only resting his eyes for a little while; instead he slept for several hours. Judging the shadows on the trees, he has only about an hour of daylight left.

The soda bottle on the ground reminds him that he has time to make a fish trap.

He rips the label off the bottle then cuts the spout large enough for small fish to swim in. After he saws the bottle in half he drops a few morsels of rice for bait then inserts the funnel inverted so it's snug. He hopes his trap works like the one he watched on a video.

He steps down to the river and places it in the water and weights it down with a rock. *That oughta do.*

****

Hidden behind a granite boulder, Brock rests his sore, aching body on a bed of pine straw and tries to get comfortable. He'd planned on reading his Bible tonight but forgot to set the solar flashlight in the sun to charge.

The final rays of daylight vanish off the mountain, and soon the hot air turns cool.

Brock digs in the pack for a blanket then tosses a couple of sticks on the glowing embers. Flames flicker and sparks pop like magic as the fire roars back to life.

Comfortably burrowed under the green wool he smiles as he recollects Buddy and his chipper, friendly manner and how blessed he was to have been rescued by him.

He caresses the cross on the leather cord around his neck and thinks of Nicole and how lovely she was and how he wished he could have gotten to know her better.

So peaceful, he thinks, staring up at the clear sky studded with thousands of twinkling stars. *I could stay here forever.*

His eyelids close, and his mind wanders to the dirty camp down the river. He tries to picture the occupants—likely a man and woman because of the swimsuits hanging on the line and a young girl because of the pink bicycle.

The old lady who threw rocks at him comes to his thoughts. *Is she the lost sheep? Is she the one the Lord sent him to find?*

CHAPTER
19

He sees a pale, silvery glimmer in the bottle trap. Three small fish swim from side to side.

Excited, Brock bends over and pulls the trap out of the water; they're too small to eat, but they will make great bait. He's hoping the campers down the river have returned so he can borrow that fishing pole.

****

"Hello? Is anybody there?" Brock surveys the dirty camp for any sign the occupants have returned.

"Hello?"

He hears a rustling sound coming from inside the tent.

"Oh, uh, sorry to bother you."

He waits.

The nylon tent shakes.

"Uh, I can come back later. I just wanted to borrow your fishing pole."

Silence.

Hmm. I guess not.

Disappointed, Brock turns to walk away when he hears a zipping noise. Stopping, he turns back to see a red-headed youth leap out of the tent, trip over a lounge chair then bolt toward the trees.

"Hey, kid! Wait up!" Brock sets the fish container on

the ground and runs after the barefooted stranger. "Wait!"

Twigs crunch under Brock's feet and branches scratch his bare arms as he chases the white T-shirt and cut-offs through the brush. Up ahead a blackberry thicket blocks the way.

"Please don't run!" Brock yells to the youth.

Trapped by the thorny vines, the teen spins around; her reddish-brown bangs are chopped off above her hard chocolate-colored eyes.

It's a girl! Brock is astonished. He was sure he was chasing a boy by the way she dressed and ran.

Her porcelain white complexion is sprinkled with freckles and stone-like with determination.

"LEAVE ME ALONE!" the girl screams, gasping for air, then charges forward like a wild animal.

Brock's strong hand snatches the thin freckled arm.

"LET ME GO!" she shrieks and kicks her bare foot at his shin. "LET ME GO!"

"Calm down, missy. I'm not gonna hurt you. I just want to borrow your fishing pole is all."

She twists her arms trying to get free. Finally she stops and pushes out her chapped, puffy lips. "You're a cop!"

"No, I'm not a cop."

"Then why are you wearing cop clothes?"

"Huh?" Brock looks down at his camo shorts. "Oh, these—a friend gave them to me. Now, please," he says in a calm but firm voice, "don't run."

He eases his grip and slowly releases her.

The girl rubs her arm, her eyes wide, her breath coming in short puffs. Finally her face softens.

A revolting smell reminds Brock of a wet dog. "I stopped by your camp yesterday, but no one was there. I'd sure like to borrow that fishing pole."

The girl gnaws at the inside of her cheek.

"I–I guess so."

"Thank you. By the way, I'm Brock. What's your name?"

"Uh." She hesitates then says, "Crystal."

****

The minnow squirms when Brock stabs it with a hook; then he tosses the line into the water. The small stick float travels downstream with the current. After waiting patiently for about ten minutes he feels a gentle tug on the line, and the stick bobs under.

Brock waits to make sure the fish has the bait in its mouth.

The line races across the water. Slowly he reels it in. He smiles when he sees a rainbow trout breach the surface and flounder. Pulling the line to shore he grasps the trout from the back and holds it firm then takes his fingers and forces the barb from its mouth.

The fish gasps.

"Sorry, little fella," Brock says under his breath. It dawns on him that he doesn't have any place to put the fish.

Think, think, he says to himself and looks around for something. He needs a bucket or bag. He rubs the back of his neck, his fingers brushing against the cord of his cross pendant. He has an idea.

Careful not to squish the trout, he holds it down with a small rock then slips off his necklace and removes the cross from the leather cord and slips it inside his shorts pocket. He ties a small twig to the end of the cord then takes the fish out from under the rock. He threads the stick through its gills and out of its mouth then ties the cord onto a low-hanging tree branch and drops the fish into the water keeping it alive until he's ready to prepare it.

Pleased with his handmade stringer, he squats down ready to retrieve another minnow when a shrill noise comes from up river. He is sure he heard someone scream.

Another sharp, piercing sound reverberates off the canyon walls and then is quickly drowned out by the rushing water.

His heart rate and blood pressure increase as he springs to his feet and rushes toward the source of the screams. He hears another scream.

As the screams get louder he catches a glimpse of red shoulder-length hair through the shrubs.

"Crystal?"

The ghost-white girl turns her head, her eyes round with fear.

"There. . .there. . .there's a bear. . . ," she stammers.

"A bear? Is that all?" He chuckles. "All that screaming and hollering over a stupid bear? It sounded like an ax-murderer was on the loose or something." He chuckles again then lowers his voice. "Okay, where's the bear?"

Crystal replies, "Behind our camp. . .at the trash pile."

Brock pulls his knife out of his shorts side pocket. "Okay, let's go find that bear."

Crystal follows close behind as they work their way to the camp.

Brock sees the blue tarp canopy ahead.

"Over there." Crystal points. "Just past the trees."

Brock crouches low, and Crystal mimics his every move. They creep past the tent and duck under the clothesline.

Grimacing from the stench, Brock grinds his teeth in revulsion as they come upon a mini-dump of trash.

Flies swarm over empty cans of food, jars and plastic containers. Refuse is piled high. A black, stout beast has his brown muzzle deep in a can.

"When I say go," Brock whispers, "wave your arms and make a lot of noise."

"What if he runs toward us?"

"Just stand still. Whatever you do, don't run. Are you ready?"

"I guess so."

"GO!"

Brock raises his arms. "HEY, YOU BEAR! SCAT! HEY! HEY, SCRAM, BEAR!"

Crystal waves her arms screaming wildly. "GO AWAY, STUPID BEAR! GO AWAY!"

The black bear pulls his snout out of the can and looks at the noise makers. His great jaw opens. "ARGHHH!"

"GO AWAY, BEAR!" Brock and Crystal yell at once, still waving their arms frantically.

One more "ARGHHH" and the bear slowly backs away then turns and shuffles into the woods.

Brock laughs out loud. "They don't call it Bear River for nothing!" He turns and starts walking back to his camp.

Crystal trots behind him. "Wait! Where you going?"

"Back to the river to catch some more fish!"

"You caught fish?"

"Yep!" Brock steps around a low-hanging tree limb. "Going to have me some fresh trout for dinner!"

Brock feels a sharp tug on the back of his shirt, stopping him.

He turns to see Crystal's lower lip pushed out and tears streaming down her cheeks.

"Please. . .please don't leave me," Crystal pleads.

"Oh, don't worry. That bear is long gone by now."

"No—I don't care about the bear." She weeps convulsively.

"What's the matter?" he asks, puzzled by the outburst.

Uneven sobs continue to shake her body.

"I can't help you if you don't tell me."

He waits patiently till the sobs turn to sniffles. "Where's your father?"

"My, my father?" She looks up, her eyes puffy and red. She sniffs then wipes her nose with the back of her hand.

"Yes, I saw a pair of men's trunks hanging on the line."

"Oh, those are JR's."

"So where's JR?"

She looks at the ground. "I don't know."

"So when is he coming back?"

"I don't know."

"How long has he been gone?"

"I don't know. . .a couple of weeks?"

"A couple of weeks?" Brock frowns.

"He went to get our monthly rations and never came back. After he left there was this *real big earthquake*."

Brock nods. "He must have been stranded in town or something. Some of the roads were destroyed, and bridges collapsed."

Crystal looks up into Brock's dark eyes, her voice suddenly sweet. "Can I come stay with you? I'm hungry."

"When was the last time you ate?"

"I don't know. . .four days ago?"

Brock's jaw drops. "You haven't eaten in four days?"

"No, and I'm hungry." Her face puckers as if she's about to cry again.

Four days? She hasn't eaten in four days? What should he do? He can feed her, but then what? He rebels at the idea of her staying with him, but he can't leave her out here alone. Besides, it might be nice to have some company.

"I guess you can stay with me at my camp till your friend shows up. I'm going to try to catch some more fish, so while I'm gone get your stuff together." He turns to walk away then stops and looks back. "Oh, can I borrow one of those white buckets to put the fish in?"

"Sure, help yourself to anything you want."

****

With his right foot Brock kicks the warm rocks away from the fire pit then fills in the gray ashes with dirt. As soon as they reach camp he fixes Crystal a beef stew a la MRE which she devours like a starving puppy.

Brock unfolds the blue-and-gray nylon material and spreads it out evenly then inserts one of the shock-corded poles into the slot. Out of the corner of his eye he notices Crystal spreading a white substance all over the ground.

What the—? He drops the pole, dashes over and yanks the bag out of Crystal's hands. "What on earth are you doing? You're making a mess."

Crystal grabs at the bag. "I'm making it so the bears won't come. Now give it back!"

Brock holds the sack high over his head.

"What are you talking about?"

"Duh, didn't you know—if you spread flour around the camp it will keep the bears away?"

"Who told you that?"

"JR—now give it back!" She swipes the air.

"Well, sorry to break it to you, missy, but the flour won't keep the bears away. In fact, it will bring the bears."

"You're lying!"

"Why would I lie? Flour is food, and bears can smell food a mile away."

Crystal's eyebrows pull together, and she takes a step back. "Why would JR lie to me?"

Brock shrugs. "Beats me."

He folds the flour sack tight and places it inside his

backpack then digs around until he produces a small, scented white bar. He turns to Crystal and holds out his hand. "Here, go take a bath. You stink."

CHAPTER

20

"Here, drink this." Brock looms over Crystal.

Crystal leans forward in the lounge chair and takes the round blue metal from Brock's hand.

"What is it?" She sniffs.

"Pine needle tea."

A scowl crosses her face. "Ewwww. I'm not drinking weeds." She pushes the cup away.

"Pine needles aren't weeds. Now drink up—you have scurvy."

"Scurvy?" Her eyes widen. "What's that? Am I going to die?"

"Not if you drink the tea. See those sores on your legs?" He points to the large purplish blotches covering her limbs. "That's because you lack vitamin C—pine needles contain vitamin C."

Crystal sighs and takes a sip of the tea. "It tastes like a Christmas tree."

"Yep."

Brock steps over to the fire and squats down. The heat warms his knees as he picks up the fork and pokes at the roasting trout.

"Looks done."

He prepares the fish and sets it on two yellow plastic plates.

"Here you go." He hands Crystal a plate then sits

down in the lounge chair next to hers. He closes his eyes. "Thank You, Lord Jesus, for this food, amen."

He rips off a small chunk of fish then sticks it in his mouth. With his tongue he feels for bones then swallows the tasty pieces without outside flavors.

"You know," Crystal says, "you're not supposed to pray to Jesus because he is only a *disciple* of Lord Maitreyas and is *not* God."

Brock stops chewing and turns toward Crystal. He discerns by the tone of her voice that she is trying to start an argument with him so he decides to ignore her comment and instead admires her hair.

Crystal snaps, "Take a picture—it'll last longer."

"I was just noticing how pretty your hair is. It reminds me of a copper penny."

"I *hate* my hair!"

Brock laughs. "By the way, I was wondering, how old are you?"

Crystal keeps her eyes focused on her plate. "I'm eighteen."

Brock senses she's lying by the look on her face. Why, she can't be more than fourteen or maybe even fifteen years old. He recalls his sister always lying about her age too. *Why do girls lie about their age?* he wonders. *When they're young they want to be old; when they're old they want to be young.*

Swallowing the last bite of trout, Brock stands and sets the plate of bones on top of a rock then pulls his Bible out of the backpack. He's looking forward to reading and relaxing; all the trips dragging supplies back and forth from Crystal's camp to his camp have worn him out.

Back in his lounge chair with his long legs outstretched and the black book in his hands, he shoots a glance over at Crystal. She is busy picking the fish off the bones on her plate.

He turns the pages to the New Testament and begins reading Matthew to himself.

"The book of the generation of Jesus Christ, the son of David, the son of Abraham—"

"What're you reading?" Crystal asks.

"The Bible."

"You know," Crystal says dramatically, "it's against the law to have a Bible. They'll kill you if you're caught with one."

"I know."

"Oh, so you're one of *them*," she charges.

Brock lifts his eyes off the page and looks at Crystal. "If you're referring to a believer in Jesus Christ, yes, I am one of *them*."

"Oh, brother." Crystal rolls her eyes in a circle. "Of all the people I get stuck with a stupid—"

"Excuse me, missy, but you're stuck with no one. If I remember right it was you who begged to come and stay with me."

"Well, that was before I knew you were one of *them*."

Brock is stern. "If you don't like me or my beliefs you can just go back down the river where you came from."

Crystal huffs. "I was just kidding. You don't have to get all mad."

Brock shakes his head, presses his lips together and then starts reading where he left off.

"Now the birth of Jesus Christ was on this wise: When as his mother Mary was espoused to Joseph, before they came together, she was found with child of the Holy Ghost—"

Crystal begins humming.

Brock ignores her.

She hums louder.

Brock is sure she is trying to annoy him; she is

succeeding.

Finally Crystal blurts out, "Will you read it out loud?"

"Yeah, sure."

Drawing in a long breath Brock makes his voice deep and clear. "Now the birth of Jesus Christ was on this wise: When as his mother—"

"No wonder they outlawed the Bible," Crystal interrupts. "Everybody knows Lord Maitreyas is the Christ, not Jesus. You're an idiot if you believe that."

Brock grits his teeth. He's had just about enough of this girl's rude behavior. He tries to keep calm, closes the Bible and bookmarks his spot with his thumb. He glowers over at the impertinent teen and says in a strong, firm voice, "As long as you're in my camp you will respect me and my beliefs, and you will NEVER refer to Maitreyas as Lord. There is only one Lord, and that is Jesus Christ—is that clear?"

Crystal crosses her arms over her chest and pushes out her lower lip.

"Is that clear?" he repeats.

"Yes," she squeaks. Mumbling, she picks up the plate from her lap, climbs across the lounge chair then stomps over and slams the yellow plastic plate on top of Brock's plate. She hastily crawls inside her tent and zips the door shut.

Brock shakes his head. *Lord, what have I gotten myself into?*

CHAPTER

21

A snapping branch zaps Brock awake. He reaches for the knife; his ears strain for sound. He has an eerie feeling he is being watched.

Soon his eyes begin to see in the dark, slightly illuminated by a half moon in the western sky.

A few minutes of nothing but a cool breeze blowing. Suddenly he hears a sharp ping as metal bangs against one of the rocks of the fire pit. Someone or something is behind Crystal's tent.

Brock leaps forward, and his heart speeds as he fumbles for the flashlight inside the backpack.

With the knife in one hand and flashlight in the other, he creeps around the side of the tent ready to pounce on the intruder.

He notices movement to the left.

Brock swings around and switches on the flashlight. Three sets of emerald-green eyes glow back at him.

Brock tries to grasp what he is seeing. *Kittens? But what would kittens be doing way out here?*

The light beam catches the black mask over their white faces. *Raccoons!* He smiles.

The three small, salt-and-pepper critters scurry after their mother and melt into the shadows.

Goosebumps emerge, and a soft wind tousles Brock's hair as he retreats back to his bed of soft pine needles. He snuggles neck-deep under his blanket.

Eyes wide open he stares up at the dark sky until the morning light peeks through the trees on top of the ridge. His lungs breathe in the chilly, crisp air; he is wide awake now. His eyes catch a flash of a yellowing aspen tree, reminding him fall is just around the corner. Fall was always his favorite time of year when the leaves changed to brilliant crimson and gold, and he would stop by Bob's Mini Mart to grab a cup of hot pumpkin spice coffee on the way to work.

He'd impress his latest girlfriend by taking her to the apple festival up at Oak Glen where they would feast on apple pie and apple donuts and split a slice of apple crisp with a scoop of vanilla ice cream.

A rumbling sound comes from deep inside his stomach. He quickly pushes food out of his thoughts and gets up; he is anxious to find the old lady down the river.

****

With the teriyaki chicken MRE tucked inside his shorts leg pocket, Brock glances over at the dome tent then quietly tiptoes out of camp, being careful not to wake Crystal.

The cold water chills his legs as he crosses the river. The long hike down the canyon and rising sun warm him.

Cautiously, he approaches Crystal's camp; he doesn't want to alarm JR if he has returned.

"Hello?"

Pause.

"Hello?"

No answer.

Rummaging through the camp, Brock fills the large plastic cooler with a few dishes, a pot, a pan, some silverware, plastic bottles and containers, and a couple of plastic buckets. He focuses on getting only things he needs for now because he can come back later, and besides, he doesn't want it to be too heavy for him to drag back to camp.

The black, five-drawer chest is stuffed with clothes. He picks out two pairs of men's white crew socks, rolls them into a ball, aims then pitches them into the ice chest. In the bottom drawer a pink and white tennis shoe is buried among the colorful tank tops and blue denim shorts. *These must be Crystal's.*

He pulls out the entire drawer and dumps all the contents into the white chest. As he walks back over to insert the drawer he notices something colorful. He reaches down and pulls out a handful of printed publications of scantily clad girls on the covers.

He fingers through the magazines, fighting the urge to read them, when one magazine catches his eye: *The Enlightened Teen.* A pretty girl with short, red, wavy hair graces the front. She reminds him of Crystal. Headlines read, "Ariana Speaks," "Bullies, How to Deal with Them," "The Right Way to Kiss," "Would You Date This Guy?" "Ten Ways. . .to Look Pretty All Summer."

Brock flips through the pages, wondering why it's mixed in with the adult magazines. He buries it in the chest then inserts the bottom drawer and closes it.

With the cooler hidden behind some rocks, Brock continues his descent into the canyon. The rising sun warms the ground. As he walks he tries to figure out how he will approach the old woman and what he'll say to her. He's prepared to get rocks thrown at him; but if he can only let her know he's friendly and means her no harm maybe she will welcome him. He plans to offer her an MRE packet then ask her if she needs any help with anything. He will follow the Lord's lead on when to share the gospel with her.

A startled young deer dashes six feet off the ground with its legs stretched straight out then speeds away.

Stopping, he mops perspiration from his face with the back of his hand. His eyes squint toward the sun as he looks at the rock dam and surveys the riverbed with keen, probing eyes searching for the old woman.

His hawk eyes scan the bank and tree-filled slope as he crosses the clear water to the other side.

Still no sign of her.

Frustrated, he drops down and leans his back against a rounded boulder, stretching his legs out in front of him. He folds his arms over his chest and listens to the water roar and the hoarse raucous sound coming from a crow.

Occasionally he swats at a fly that buzzes around his eyes. The day warms up quickly as the sun moves overhead.

A small ground squirrel hurries past him with an acorn in his mouth. Brock watches in awe as it stops, digs a hole and drops the nut inside; then he carefully covers the nut with the soil and pats it down. The squirrel looks back over his shoulder toward the buried acorn as he hurries away, probably to find another one, Brock guesses. The squirrel is gathering nuts for the winter; that's what he should be doing instead of sitting here wasting time doing nothing.

Restless, he starts thinking of all the things he needs to do back at camp. And Crystal—she's probably been up for hours wondering where he is.

He stands. He'll come back in a few days and try again.

****

Crystal squats down on a rock hugging her knees; she's staring at the water. The white threads of her cutoffs run down her legs, and her pink tank top brings out the brilliant copper color in her hair. Brock takes notice.

"Hey, Copperhead!" he shouts as he works his way toward her.

Crystal turns, stands and crosses her arms over her chest. "What took you so long?" She glowers at him. "I've been waiting for you for hours."

Brock plunks the ice chest on the rounded pebbles.

"Where were you?" Her eyebrows are furrowed. "I heard someone outside my tent, and you weren't there."

"Oh, those were raccoons."

"No. . .I *heard* footsteps," she persists.

"You *thought* you heard footsteps. A family of raccoons wandered in our camp last night. I scared them away. After that I couldn't go back to sleep so I got up early to see if I could catch that old lady down the—"

"What old lady?" She puts her hands on her hips.

"There's an old lady down the river, a few miles below your camp."

"Do you mean the old hag?"

"I'm not sure."

"The one with the stringy gray hair?"

"I think that's her. Do you know her?"

"She's mean. I was minding my own business when she started throwing rocks at me. . .stupid hag. . . ."

"Yep." Brock chuckles. "That's her all right! So what did you do?"

"I threw them back." Crystal rolls her eyes. "Like who's she to tell me not to trespass? Ha! It's like she thinks she owns the whole river or something."

She brushes back a stray lock from her eyes. "So what do you want with that old hag?"

Brock has decided no way is he going to tell Crystal his motive for finding the old lady so he quickly changes the subject.

"I have a job for you!"

"Huh?"

"I said I have a job for you!"

Plastic creaks as Brock raises the lid of the cooler.

"JR's gonna kill you for stealing all his stuff!"

"What?" Brock looks up then back down in the chest. "I'm not stealing JR's stuff. Besides, you said I could borrow anything I needed. Here." He pulls out a white five-gallon bucket and sets it on the rocks in front of her. "I want you to fill up this bucket with acorns, and when you're finished I have a surprise for you."

"A surprise?" Crystal's eyes light up, and the corners of her mouth quirk upward. "Really? A surprise. What is it?"

"It wouldn't be a surprise if I told you now. I'll give it to you when you're done."

Her smile vanishes. "What are the acorns for?"

"To eat!"

"You're gonna eat them?"

"No. . .*we're* going to eat them. Did you know a handful of acorns is as nutritious as a pound of hamburger?"

"No."

"How do you think the Indians survived around here?"

"I don't know. So how come we have to eat acorns? Why can't we just eat those food pouch things?"

"Because we're saving the MREs for emergencies."

A few hours later Crystal groans as she sets the bucket on the ground. "Where's my surprise?"

Brock climbs out of the lounge chair. "We're not finished yet."

"But you said when I filled up the bucket I could have my surprise," she argues.

"I meant when we're done."

"Oh, brother." Her eyes roll.

Brock picks up the pail by the handle. "Grab that

saucepan over there—oh, and that cup too." He nods toward the dishes. "And follow me."

Clutching the cup and saucepan, Crystal follows Brock down to the river's edge. She stands and watches him dip the bucket into the current and fill it up with water.

"Hey! Hey!" Crystal admonishes him. "You're losing the acorns—they're floating away!"

"Those are rotten; we want them to float away."

"Oh."

Brock swooshes the nuts around in the bucket picking out the floating ones. When he's finished he drains the water and steps to shore.

"Are we done? Can I have my surprise?"

"No. Hand me that cup."

Crystal huffs then hands Brock the blue plastic.

Brock dips it into the bucket. "I want you to take this bucket up to camp and spread the rest of the acorns out on a towel to dry in the sun. Your job is to keep an eye on them and make sure no animals get our acorns." He looks up. "Do you think you can handle that?"

"Yeah, whatever. Then do I get my surprise?"

"Hold on, missy." He holds out the cup. "We still have to shell, leach and cook these."

"Oh, brother," Crystal mumbles.

As Brock steps into the water to fill the saucepan he sees a large black mass dangling between the rocks below the falls.

"I'll be back in a second."

He drops the saucepan on the gravel and peels his T-shirt over his head. He removes the cross necklace then wades into the water.

A cold blast hits him as he lowers himself into the fast-moving current. Keeping his head above the water, he swims the sidestroke. His strong arms and legs pull him through the white water toward the dark mass.

A body. Brock's heart stutters. Two stiff limbs are wedged between the rocks.

He maneuvers around the boulder to get a better look. With his fingertips he hoists himself up onto the hard surface. His chest drums louder than the water plummeting over the three-tiered falls.

The corpse is face down. Brock notices a patch on the shirt and instantly recognizes the gold pyramid surrounded by ten stars as if it is branded in his brain: "World Union—Novus Ordo Seclorum—A New Order for the Ages."

Smitty?

He pulls the black sleeve toward him.

The head rolls over revealing a blue-faced man; his mouth is wide open in a frozen scream; his eyes are gouged out, and part of his skull is missing.

Ugh. Brock pulls back from the gruesome sight, slightly disappointed that it isn't Smitty.

If the dead guy is a cop he most likely has a tracking device, and the authorities will come looking for him.

The thought of cops scouring the canyon for a body sends a shiver through him. He needs to get rid of the body and quick.

What if he buries it?

Bad idea. They'll track and find the body and realize "someone" buried it and probably look for that person. The best option he can think of is for him to swim the body down the river as far from their camp as possible, and maybe the current will take him all the way to Sacramento.

Then another frightening thought surfaces: If someone killed the cop and dumped him in the river, a killer is on the loose. He decides he must deal with first things first and get rid of the body.

He slips back into the water.

"BROCK!" Crystal yells. "What's taking you so long? What is it?"

Ignoring Crystal, Brock swims around the boulder and grabs the bottom of the black trousers and tugs.

The body doesn't budge.

Another tug.

The rock is stubborn and won't release its victim, like a Venus fly trap snaring a bug. He draws in a deep breath, holds it and dives under the surface.

With both hands he grasps the dead man's ankles, plants both his feet against the boulder and pushes off as hard as he can.

The rock finally yields, and the body crashes into the water sending a tsunami of waves.

Brock releases one ankle and swims to the surface gasping for air. He tightens his grip on the other ankle as the swift current carries them down toward a series of rapids. He glances up in time to see Crystal's mouth gaping open as the two men float by. She starts running along the shoreline.

"Brock!" she yells.

"Stay there!" he commands. With all of his strength Brock holds the man's ankle tight as they shoot down the first set of rapids.

The river fights Brock for the body, but he hangs on. The two continue down the river.

He hears the loud rumbling as they approach another set of rapids. Brock fights to hang on to the corpse in a tug of war; but the raging water finally wins and rips the body out of his hand.

Water smacks hard against Brock's face, as though the river is punishing him. It spins and bounces him like a washing machine then sucks him under. He loses all sense of up or down and continues to hold his breath as he is plunges through the rapids. No longer is he battling the river for the corpse—but for his own life.

Help me, Lord! he cries silently.

His body slams against a flat rock; his aching fingers manage to hang on.

Coughing and sputtering he fills his lungs with air then swims around the rock and hauls his bruised body to shore. He has survived.

****

Trying to forget about the dead cop in the river, Brock smashes the outer covering of the acorn shell with a rock, breaking it into small pieces. He's mad at himself for not getting that hammer from JR's tool box. He'll have to get it when he goes back down again.

Crystal had pestered him with a million questions about the "dead guy." He didn't tell her it was a cop—just told her some guy had probably fallen in and drowned. She seemed satisfied with his explanation.

Crystal pops a shelled acorn into her mouth. Her face twists and her mouth puckers before she spits it out.

"Ewww, they taste nasty!"

"That's because we haven't leached them yet."

"What's that mean?"

"It means we have to get the tannin out. That's what makes them taste so bitter. The Indians used to soak them in the river for a few days, but we're going to cheat and boil the tannin out."

"Oh."

Brock places the nuts on a flat rock and begins smashing the white meat with another rock, grinding them into coarse meal.

"You see, this is how the Indians did it. Sometimes you can find holes worn in the rocks where they pounded the acorns. They're called grinding stones."

"Are you an Indian or something?"

"No, what makes you say that?"

"Because it seems like you know an awful lot about Indians."

"I just read books on survival is all."

"Oh."

Brock scoops up the ground nuts then drops them back into the cup.

"Here, you can carry this." He passes the cup to Crystal.

"Why do I have to carry everything?"

"Because I'm going to carry the saucepan with water. Would you rather carry that?"

"No. "

****

Back at camp Crystal sits on a small boulder; her elbows are propped on her knees, and her chin rests in her palms. She watches as Brock lights a fire then sets the pot on the flame. When the water hisses and bubbles, Brock dumps the cup of coarse meal into the pot and waits till the water darkens then takes the pan off the fire and pours the brown water into several empty plastic soda containers.

"What's that for?" Crystal asks.

"It's tannin. The Indians used it to tan their hides to make clothes."

Crystal gives her usual response. "Oh."

"You can use it for laundry soap too, and it is also an antiviral and can be used as an antiseptic. When the water cools I'll rub some on those sores on your legs from the scurvy."

Brock adds fresh water to the nuts and keeps boiling

and changing the water until the water is clear. When he's finished he dumps the water and waits for the mush to cool then forms several small balls out of the moist dough and lets them sit for about ten minutes. He then flattens them into patties and places them in the frying pan over the fire, cooking both sides till they are slightly brown.

The smell of burning wood and roasting nuts floods the camp. Taking a fork, Brock jabs two of the acorn cakes and sets them on a plate.

"Here—you can have one now. We'll save the rest for dinner."

Crystal accepts the snack and scoots back into the lounge chair. She sniffs the hard, brown cake. "Do they taste good?"

Sitting down in the lounge next to her, he takes a bite. "Not bad. . .it tastes like boiled chestnuts!"

Crystal nibbles the edge of her patty.

"Your job is to fill a bucket of acorns every day, remove the rotten ones like I showed you and lay them out in the sun to dry. Do you think you can handle that?"

"Yeah, whatever."

Her eyes suddenly light up, and she turns to Brock. "Where's my surprise?"

"It's in the bottom of the ice chest."

Setting the plate down, Crystal hurries over to the cooler. A big smile lights her face as she digs around for her surprise. Suddenly her eyes bug out. "Wow! Cool! Where'd you get this?"

Not waiting for an answer she stumbles back to the lounge chair and sits down, staring at the cover of the teen magazine.

Brock laughs. "Oh, I almost forgot—I have something else you might like. Go in the side pocket of the backpack—it should be in there."

Crystal drops the magazine on the chair, hurries over to the camouflage pack and unzips several pockets till she locates a round silver tube.

"Is this it?" She holds it up.

He smiles. "Yes, that's it."

Popping the lid off, she beams. "LIPSTICK! You got me lipstick!"

CHAPTER

22

With the shovel balanced on the lid Brock picks up the chest by the side handles. He yells down at the tent, "I'll be back in a few hours!"

"Wait!" A fast zipping sound then copper hair pokes through the tent's door. Crystal squints from the bright morning sunlight.

"Where you going?"

"To catch a squirrel."

She looks at the shovel and white ice chest.

"How're you gonna do that?"

Brock thinks for a second. "I'm going to put the chest over my head then dance around and act like a nut. When the squirrel comes, I'm going to whack him over the head with the shovel."

Her face clouds for a second then clears. "Ha! Ha! Very funny." Her head dips back behind the blue nylon fabric.

Brock chuckles as he steps away.

The morning sun beats down on his back, and his lungs fill with a sweet, pine-scented aroma as he climbs the hill behind the camp. He gazes past the spiky top of a young Ponderosa pine toward the giant oaks. A sense of serenity fills his soul as he progresses up the hill. He stops under an aging oak tree, its sprawling, low-hanging branches covered with burley leaves and ripening acorns.

This looks like a good place.

Brock drops the shovel and lowers the chest to the ground.

Crouching, he raises the lid and pulls out the spoon, the aluminum can full of shelled acorns mixed with rice and the slender piece of wood he'd found along the way. He turns the chest upside down and props it open with the stick. Carefully he places the spoon full of the acorn and rice inside the chest, balancing the flat part under the stick.

That oughta do.

He stands.

Carrying the shovel over his shoulder, he bounds back down the slope keeping his eyes peeled for a place to dig a spider hole. He wants to be prepared in case someone comes looking for that dead cop—so he and Crystal will have a place to hide.

A clearing next to some shrubs catches his eye. It has a good view of the camp—he can see Crystal sitting on the lounge looking at her magazine.

Brock drops the shovel and sticks it in the dirt.

Sweat forms on his forehead as he shovels and piles the soil into a large mound. Scooping the soft earth, he wonders when JR will return and what he'll do when he finds Crystal gone. He hopes JR is friendly but reminds himself that he must be cautious and have a backup plan in case he's not. Buddy had warned him about the bounty placed on resisters' heads. They're "wanted dead or alive" by the American Union police. People are so desperate to survive they will turn in family members for credits for food and supplies.

Standing back, Brock admires the four-foot by two-and-a-half-foot hole. He'd placed two large rocks in front and spread foliage around to break up the outline. Now all he needs to do is line the bottom of the hole with pine straw.

Brock purposely ignores the blue jay jeering at him from above as he trudges his way through the thick brush toward a tall timber laden with lush, green needles.

He is suddenly startled by a storm of buzzing, crackling sounds flooding the air.

RATTLESNAKE!

Brock stops with a jolt. His throat tightens, and adrenaline courses through his veins.

Frantically he searches the ground.

A heavy-bodied serpent is coiled a few feet away. Its triangular-shaped head is low, hissing and whipping its narrow forked tongue between its poisonous fangs. The rattles continue to warn with a sinister, insistent SHHHHHHHH as its tail shakes back and forth rapidly.

Help me, Lord! Brock pleads, afraid to move.

Cold sweat oozes from his forehead.

He recalls when he was a kid and used to go dirt-bike riding with his friend Eddie up in Frazier Park. They came across a rattlesnake sunning itself in the middle of the trail, and Eddie killed it with a big rock.

Out of the corner of his eye Brock spots a rock. Careful not to make any sudden gesture, he slowly moves his right foot backward then bends his knees. His hand inches down the back of his leg till he reaches the ground and feels the rock. He grasps it as though his life depends on it. Quietly he stands straight then lifts the rock high over his head.

Please, Lord, don't let me miss.

With full force he hurls the rock at the snake aiming straight for the head.

SMACK!

The reptile flips over and over, its scaly body twisting from side to side.

Brock grabs another rock and repeats the blows until he's sure the snake is dead.

Feeling the side of his shorts he realizes he forgot his knife back at camp so he finds a stick and pins down the serpent's head. With the sharp end of a rock he pounds off the poisonous head then buries it and places a large rock on top to keep the animals from eating it.

Still shaken, Brock picks up the serpent decorated with dark diamond shapes along its back and starts walking.

"HEY, COPPERHEAD! COME HERE!" he yells toward the camp.

As he approaches the spider hole he looks down at the lounge chair; Crystal hasn't moved.

"HEY, COPPERHEAD. . .COME UP HERE! I WANNA SHOW YOU SOMETHING. . .AND BRING MY KNIFE."

He wonders what's taking her so long. Finally he sees red hair bobbing through the bushes.

"UP HERE!" he shouts to get her attention.

Face red, she yells back, "QUIT CALLING ME COPPERHEAD! A copperhead is a disgusting snake."

"What?" Brock grins, hiding his hand behind his back. "You don't like snakes?"

"I HATE snakes!" she snarls. "The only good snake is a DEAD snake!"

"Well, good, then—you'll like what's for dinner." Nonchalantly he pulls out his hand from behind his back revealing the six-foot-long rattlesnake.

"AHHHHHHH!" Crystal lets out an ear-piercing scream.

"What?" Brock teases. "It's a *good* snake, remember? You said the only *good* snake is a dead snake!"

"Ewww. It's gross!" Her nose wrinkles in disgust.

"I'm sorry," Brock says with a boyish grin. "I just couldn't resist."

His voice becomes serious. "Here. . .hand me my knife."

Crystal extends her hand as far from her as she can to pass him the blade. She watches Brock stretch the reptile out on the ground when suddenly the decapitated snake strikes at Brock's arm.

"It's still alive!" she screams and jumps backward. "It's still alive!"

Remaining calm Brock replies, "No, it's just nerves."

"Are you sure?" She takes a cautious step forward.

"Yes, I'm sure."

Brock chops off the rattles. "Here." He tosses them in Crystal's direction.

Out of his eye he watches her pick them up and shake them back and forth. He smiles to himself.

"Wanna help me skin him?" He knows the answer but is amused by her fear over the silly dead snake. He wonders why girls are so afraid of snakes. Why, even his aunt Millie—he thought she would have a heart attack when a little gopher snake tried to get into their house from their back patio. He picked it up and released it into a field down the street.

"No way." Crystal turns to leave.

"Oh, wait. . .I almost forgot."

"What?"

Brock stands up then points his knife toward the freshly shoveled mound of dirt.

Crystal eyeballs the hole. "What's that for?"

"That is called a spider hole."

"A spider hole?"

"Yes. Now when I'm gone and you hear someone, I want you to run up here and hide in this hole and cover yourself with that branch." He points to the branch.

Crystal frowns, and her face turns red. "Why do you have to call it a spider hole?"

"Because that's what it's called. . .a spider hole! It's a

small fox hole the military uses for hiding or observation."

"But I HATE SPIDERS!"

"I don't care what you call it. Call it a rabbit hole or a flower hole. The point is, when someone comes near here I want you to go hide in it."

He shakes his head in frustration and says under his breath, "Ungrateful brat."

"What did you say?"

"Never mind."

CHAPTER

23

For as the lightning cometh out of the east, and shineth even unto the west; so shall also the coming of the Son of man be.
Matthew 24:27

"It does taste like chicken." Crystal chews then swallows the snake meat.

"Yep, I told you so."

Crystal looks over at Brock sitting in the lounge next to her.

"Where did you get it?"

Brock points his head over his shoulder. "He was sunning himself beyond those trees over there. I almost stepped on him."

He fingers another piece of meat and pops it in his mouth. "You really need to be careful. That rattler may have a mate so keep your eyes and ears open."

Glancing at the black flip-flops dangling from Crystal's feet he adds, "And you need to wear your tennis shoes when walking through the brush."

"Did you hear me?"

"No, what did you say?"

"I said," he says, raising his voice, "be careful. More rattlesnakes may be around. I want you to wear your tennis shoes when walking through the brush."

"You don't have to be so mean about it."

"I wasn't trying to be mean. I just want you to understand that if you get bit by a rattlesnake you'll probably have zero chance of survival."

"Yeah, whatever."

Crystal licks her fingers. "I don't get it."

"What don't you get?"

"How come you hunt for food like some wild man? Why don't you just get monthly rations like everybody else?"

"Because I won't take the mark of the beast."

Crystal's brows pull together. "What's that?"

"Maitreyas is the beast, and I won't take his mark."

"I still don't get it."

"You can't get monthly rations without Maitreyas's mark. The Bible says Maitreyas is the beast and if you take his mark you'll go to hell and be tortured by fire and brimstone."

"Really? The Bible says that?"

"Yes, it says all who take his mark and worship him will suffer God's wrath. It gives clues to who the beast is, and from the clues it's Maitreyas."

Brock climbs out of the chair, sets the empty plate on a rock then fetches his Bible. Returning to the chair, he opens the book to Revelation 13 and reads aloud: "'And he causeth all—.'" Brock stops and explains to Crystal, "He is referring to the false prophet."

Then he continues reading: "'And he causeth all, both small and great, rich and poor, free and bond, to receive a mark in their right hand, or in their foreheads: And that no man might buy or sell, save he that had the mark, or the name of the beast, or the number of his name. Here is wisdom. Let him that hath understanding count the number of the beast: for it is the number of a man; and his number is six hundred threescore and six' [Revelation 13:16-18].

"Not only does Maitreyas's name equal 666 in Greek and Hebrew, but he fulfills every prophecy concerning the antichrist in the Bible. Maitreyas is the beast John warned about."

He flips the pages. "Here's what happens to those who take the mark." Brock clears his throat. "'And the third angel followed them, saying with a loud voice, If any man worship the beast and his image, and receive his mark in his forehead, or in his hand, the same shall drink of the wine of the wrath of God, which is poured out without mixture into the cup of his indignation; and he shall be tormented with fire and brimstone in the presence of the holy angels, and in the presence of the Lamb: and the smoke of their torment ascendeth up for ever and ever: and they have no rest day nor night, who worship the beast and his image, and whosoever receiveth the mark of his name. Here is the patience of the saints: here *are* they that keep the commandments of God, and the faith of Jesus'" [Revelation 14:9-12].

Crystal's brows wrinkle. She looks down at her hands and inspects them. "Do I have the mark of the beast?"

"Did you bow down and worship an image of Maitreyas and take the Luciferian oath?"

"No."

"Did you get a chip implant?"

"No, JR said I didn't need one."

"Then you don't have the mark of the beast."

The wrinkles disappear, and she lets out a long breath. "So how come Peter Roma makes everyone get a mark?"

"For one thing it's to trick people into thinking Maitreyas is God—"

"How does a mark trick people?"

"The Bible says the one true God marks His children

with a sign of ownership and puts His name on their foreheads. It's a spiritual mark so it's invisible to the naked eye. Maitreyas is pretending to be God, so that's why he's putting his mark and name on people. Here. . .let me see if I can find it."

Brock skims the verses then reads, "'And they shall see his face'—it's talking about God's face—'and his name shall be in their foreheads' [Revelation 22:4].

"This particular verse is talking about the new heaven and new earth when the believers see Father God in all His glory. And the reason you can't buy or sell without the mark? It's to make it difficult for resisters to survive."

"JR said the Bible was written by men so I bet it doesn't mean that at all."

"The Bible is the inspired Word of God—in other words, God inspired men to write down His words. And think about it, Crystal: John had these visions more than two thousand years ago. Peter Roma outlawed the Bible and replaced it with a twisted version because he didn't want people to know the truth."

Crystal leans back. "So what is the truth?"

"Jesus is the truth! The Bible says He is the way, the truth and the life, and no one goes to God except through Him."

"But JR said Peter Roma is Jesus reincarnated."

"No, Peter Roma is the false prophet, the second beast of Revelation. Remember what I just read in Revelation? Jesus Christ, the real Jesus, ascended to heaven and is preparing a place for the believers to join Him. Before He left He told His disciples that many would come in His name and claim to be Him or the Christ. He said not to believe it because He was coming back in the sky, 'as lightning flashes from east to west'" [Revelation 14:9-12].

Brock waits silently as he watches Crystal soak

everything up like a sponge.

"So how do we get the real God's mark on our forehead?"

"When you accept Jesus and confess that He is the Lord and believe in your heart that God raised Him from the dead, you'll be saved. When you repent of your sins, He'll forgive you. That's when the Holy Spirit marks your forehead."

Brock opens the Bible and turns the pages then stops. "'In whom ye also *trusted*, after that ye heard the word of truth, the gospel of your salvation: in whom also after that ye believed, ye were sealed with that holy Spirit of promise'" [Ephesians 1:13].

Brock closes his Bible and leans toward Crystal. He looks deep into her eyes. "Would you like to accept Jesus as your Lord and Savior?"

"Don't push it," Crystal snaps.

Disappointed Brock says, "I can't make you accept Jesus because God gives you free will; you can either accept Him or reject Him. But I will pray for you, Crystal, that the Holy Spirit will guide you to the truth."

"Whatever—"

"Shh!" Brock holds up his hand and listens.

Whump-whump-whump. The rhythmic sound of a helicopter wings its way down the river canyon.

Brock catches his breath, his pulse racing. *The dead cop.*

"QUICK! Go hide in the spider hole!"

"What for?"

"COPS!"

Brock lurches to his feet, and Crystal scrambles out of the chair.

The fire! He kicks dirt over the glowing embers then kicks apart the circle of stones.

Now the tent! No time to drag it under the trees! He unlocks the corded poles and pulls them out of their sockets. The tent collapses like a deflated beach ball. He folds the lounge chairs and hurls them on top of the tent.

The constant whump-whump-whump ricocheting off the canyon walls stabs Brock's core. His heart accelerates as he rushes around the camp piling all their belongings on the tent—the plastic bucket, the plates.

Almost tossing the Bible in the pile, he stops. If they find it they'll know they're resisters and send police or even the military to look for them.

He drops to his knees and yanks the blanket out of the backpack, stuffing the Bible inside. Then he spreads the green fabric over the heap of camping gear, camouflaging it.

With the backpack tight in his hand, he races up the hill toward the spider hole when a voice in his head screams, *"THE FLASHLIGHT!"*

Dropping the backpack he wheels around, and then like a Navy SEAL on a special reconnaissance mission he bounds back down the hill and dives behind the boulder.

His damp hands snatch the black plastic charging in the sun.

The *whump–whump–whump* thunders through the canyon as the chopper creeps toward them.

Inhaling two deep breaths, Brock dashes from the covering of the boulder and runs like a scared jack rabbit with a coyote on his heels to the spider hole.

He tosses his backpack into the pit then slides down next to Crystal.

Shaking, he drags the pine branches over their heads, concealing their location.

"What took you so long?" Crystal's whisper sounds agitated.

"I forgot the solar flashlight. I had to go back and get

it—the reflection might have given us away."

Crystal nods then peeks through the branches. "I wonder what they're doing?"

Whump–whump–whump. The helicopter moves toward them. Brock holds his breath, sweat dripping from his head and arms. He prays they don't notice the square outline of his blanket at the camp.

He recalls the last time he was hiding from a helicopter—in the shed with Arthur and Jesse—and that didn't end well.

Sweat dribbles down his forehead as he peers through the branches. He can see the co-pilot gazing down at the water.

"Stay down!" He jerks his head back and sinks lower into the pit.

Whump–whump–whump. The chopper hums loudly as it passes by.

The chopper makes a sharp turn and circles overhead then lowers itself, making a hovering sound.

Peering through the branches again Brock looks for the chopper; it's hidden from view.

"What are they doing?"

"Don't know." He slinks back down into the hole.

The two of them wait.

It seems as if they are there for hours when the helicopter suddenly rises above the treeline. Brock can see an orange rescue basket dangling underneath it. *They've recovered the body.*

The chopper ascends high above the ridge then zips westward.

Brock lets out a loud sigh. *That was close.*

He pushes the branches aside and climbs out of their hiding place then stoops over and gives Crystal a hand out.

"What was that basket thing for?" Crystal brushes

pine needles off her seat.

"To haul the dead guy."

"Oh, you mean they found that dead guy? Well, he must have been pretty important for all that big deal over him."

"That was a pretty smart observation, Copperhead."

"Why do you say that?"

"The dead guy—he was a cop."

CHAPTER

24

"Copperhead, have you filled up a bucket of acorns yet?" Brock stares down at the teen. Her long white legs are stretched out on the chair, and her eyes are buried in her magazine.

Crystal looks up with rose-painted lips. Ignoring Brock's question she puckers up her mouth. "Am I pretty?"

"You could be."

"What's that supposed to mean?"

"If you'd wear a smile instead of a frown all the time you'd be very pretty." He pauses then continues. "It doesn't matter how much makeup a girl puts on, as long as she wears a scowl on her face, it's a turn off. But when a girl smiles it warms a guy's heart and makes her very pretty."

"What-ever." Crystal drops her eyes back down to her magazine.

"Now have you filled up a bucket of acorns yet?"

"No."

"It's getting late. You need to go fill up the bucket; you can read your magazine later."

Crystal folds her arms over her chest. "I don't want to—I'm tired of picking up acorns."

Here we go again. Another childish outburst— just when I was starting to warm up to her.

"You don't work—you don't eat," he says firmly.

"Who says?"

"I do."

A loud huff then comes that disdainful eye roll. "Oh, brother, I'll bet your stupid Bible says that too."

Brock presses his lips together. *I don't need this. God sent me on a mission to find that old lady, not to babysit an ungrateful brat.*

"Listen here, missy. I've had just about enough of your bad mouthing the Word of God, and I'm sick and tired of your attitude. Tomorrow you go back to your camp and wait for your friend."

"But—"

"No buts. The first thing in the morning I'm taking you back."

A look of horror fills her face.

"Don't worry." Brock's voice softens. "I'll check on you every day and bring you food till your friend shows up."

"But I can't go back!" she pleads, her eyes wide. "JR will kill me."

Now it's Brock's turn to roll his eyes. He knows she is playing her favorite role as drama queen, but he decides to let her perform. He sits down in the lounge chair and faces her. "Okay, so why would JR kill you?"

"JR"—she slowly spits out the words—"JR. . .is not my friend."

Brock stands to his feet. "I don't care if he's your dad, brother or uncle—first thing in the morning you're out of here."

"No, wait. . .you don't understand. I. . .uh. . . ." Suddenly she blurts out, "JR KIDNAPPED ME!"

Brock gasps then slowly turns around. "You're not joking with me, are you, Crystal?"

"No." She looks him in the eye then down at the ground. "I promise."

"You were kidnapped?" He repeats it almost as if he's

making sure he'd heard her right.

"Yes."

It feels as if he's been socked him in the stomach. *Crystal was kidnapped?*

"I'm so sorry, Crystal. I had no idea."

He sits on the chair next to hers. *So Crystal was kidnapped? Wow! This changes everything. I can't take her back now, or ever. What should I do? I wasn't planning to take care of anyone. I'm on a mission from God. I'll just have to figure it out later.*

"So what happened?"

Crystal takes the edge of her shirt and wipes the moisture around her eyes.

"I was eleven." She draws in a long breath. "I was walking to the bus stop when this black truck pulled over and this guy, it was JR, he asked me for directions to the school. He said he'd just moved into the area and wanted to register his daughter there. He seemed like a nice man so I told him where the school was. He thanked me and offered me a ride, but I said no because I knew Mom would kill me if I took a ride from a stranger.

"Then he held up this weird device thing. The next thing I know, I'm on the ground and can't move. I was numb all over. . .he'd zapped me with a stun gun. He picked me up and threw me onto the floor of his truck then covered me up with a blanket."

It's gut-wrenching for Brock to listen to Crystal tell her story; deep inside he fears the worst.

"He drove for a while then pulled over and put this gray tape over my mouth and taped my hands and feet."

Brock visualizes a frightened, skinny, red-headed girl with duct tape over her mouth shoved onto the floorboard of a truck. His heart aches.

"When we got to his house he hid me in the blanket

and carried me inside. He handcuffed me to a bed where I stayed for months, maybe longer." She looks down at her feet. "It seemed like years."

"Eventually we left that place, and that's when we started camping."

He didn't dare ask her if JR abused her physically, but he knew. Poor Crystal. No wonder she always seemed so unhappy.

His own anger swells as he envisions the terror she must have felt, snatched from the loving arms of her family and chained to a bed like an animal. *If I ever get my hands on the monster I'll kill him—*. A voice interrupts his thoughts. *"Vengeance is mine, saith the Lord."*

"Did you ever try to get away?"

"No. I was scared, so I did everything he told me to do 'cuz he said he would kill me if I didn't."

Brock reaches over and puts his hand on hers. "I'm so sorry you had to go through that." He adds, "I won't take you back. You can stay here."

Recompense to no man evil for evil. Provide things honest in the sight of all men. If it be possible, as much as lieth in you, live peaceably with all men. Dearly beloved, avenge not yourselves, but rather give place unto wrath: for it is written, Vengeance is mine; I will repay, saith the Lord. Therefore if thine enemy hunger, feed him; if he thirst, give him drink: for in so doing thou shalt heap coals of fire on his head. Be not overcome of evil, but overcome evil with good.
Romans 12:17-21

CHAPTER

25

"Guess what?" Brock is in a cheerful mood as he steps to the river's edge.

Knee deep in water, hunched over a bucket, Crystal glances his way then stands straight, a blank expression on her face. She puts her hands on her hips. "What?"

Brock cannot conceal his excitement. "We're going to have squirrel for dinner!"

"Oh. . .that's nice."

Brock detects something is wrong.

"Do you want to know how I caught it?"

"I guess so."

Crystal crosses her arms over her chest as the water gently slaps against her legs.

"Remember the ice chest? I made a trap out of it! Funny thing is, I got the idea from when I was a kid. A mouse was in my mom's bathtub—"

"Was there water in it?"

"Oh, no, if water was in the tub the poor mouse would have drowned. Anyway my mom was scared of the mouse, and I didn't want to kill it so I made a trap. I set my lunch box upside down in the tub with the lid on the bottom then propped it open with a fork. I spread peanut butter on a cracker and put it on a spoon and balanced the flat end under the bottom of the fork. About five minutes later I heard the lid shut so I ran into my mom's bathroom, and sure enough that little mouse tripped the spoon and was trapped inside my lunch box!"

"Oh, that's nice."

Crystal bends over, dunks her hands back into the bucket and swirls the acorns around.

Brock was sure she would have laughed or at least smiled at his story.

"Crystal, is everything okay?"

She stares down at the brown nuts. "Yeah."

He's sure it isn't.

"What's wrong, Crystal?"

She frowns. "Nothing."

"Come on—tell me what happened."

Brock wades into the water and pulls out the bucket, setting it on the shoreline.

Crystal follows him and sits down on the gravel. She hugs her knees to her chest and stares straight ahead.

Brock drops down next to her. He searches her face. "Okay, spill it—tell me what's wrong."

"Nothing."

"Now I know something is wrong. I'm not leaving here until you tell me."

She shrugs. "I had a bad dream last night, that's all."

"So what was it about?"

"I was in this big city." She turns toward Brock. "Hundreds of people were running and screaming, and I looked up and saw these great big fireballs falling from the sky. Some of them were as big as cars. The fireballs were slamming against buildings and catching everything on fire. Then the fireballs started hitting people and knocking them on the ground. People were yelling and screaming. This one guy, I remember him clearly, his clothes were smoking and on fire, and his skin was burning, and he was cursing at God. I was so scared and started running. I didn't know where to go—the fireballs were hitting everywhere.

"Then I saw this old man. He wasn't afraid at all. He just walked calmly up to me and said, 'Why are you so afraid, my child?'

"He reminded me of a prophet.

"I yelled at him. 'Are you blind? Can't you see people are dying and burning up alive?'

"Then he said the strangest thing, Brock. 'They perish because they took the mark of the beast and rejected the love of the truth that they might be saved.' And then he said, 'The time is short, my child. You must choose *this* day whom you will serve, Jesus Christ of Nazareth or the beast.' And then I woke up."

Brock's eyes widen. He stares across the river as he visualizes Crystal's dream. It is as though she was transported into the future when the fourth angel pours his bowl out on the sun, causing it to scorch with fire the people who had taken the mark of the beast.

His hand rubs the stubble on his chin.

Crystal interrupts his thoughts. "It was so real, Brock. I was so scared. . . ."

Brock turns back toward her and looks deep into her eyes as though he is looking straight into her soul. "Crystal, so whom do you choose, Jesus or Maitreyas?"

"I–I don't know. . . ." Her eyes lower.

"You must choose, Crystal. . .today."

"But why do I have to choose today? I want more time to think about it."

"Because the old man in your dream said you must choose today."

Crystal groans and looks down at the ground then shifts uneasily.

Brock continues to stare silently as he prays for her. He knows a spiritual battle is taking place as the devil fights with resolute resistance to losing grasp of Crystal's soul.

He holds his breath as she raises her eyes to meet his.

"I—I choose Jesus, Brock," she blurts out. "I don't want to die and go to hell. I want to go to heaven and be with Him and you!"

Water wells up in Brock's eyes. Joy floods his soul.

"Praise the Lord!" he utters under his breath.

His muscular arms grasp her tiny shoulders, and he squeezes her in a gentle embrace. "Praise the Lord," he repeats over and over. "Praise the Lord."

That if thou shalt confess with thy mouth the Lord Jesus, and shalt believe in thine heart that God hath raised him from the dead, thou shalt be saved. For with the heart man believeth unto righteousness; and with the mouth confession is made unto salvation.
Romans 10:9-10

CHAPTER
26

Humming to himself, Brock stuffs the teriyaki chicken MRE into the pocket of his camo shorts then zips the backpack shut. He glances over at Crystal who's wearing an oversized white tank top and blue jean cutoffs, sitting on the lounge chair, looking into a mirror and rubbing her fingers across her forehead. He's amazed at the sudden change in her personality; it's as though she has been transformed into a different person.

"Watcha doin, Copperhead?"

"I can't see it, Brock."

"See what?"

"God's name on my forehead." She continues to stare at her reflection.

Brock chuckles. "Silly, I told you it's a spiritual mark. Humans can't see it—only those in the spirit world can see it."

She turns from the mirror to Brock.

"Do you mean like angels? Do you think they can see it?"

"Oh, yes, I'm sure of it, and demons can see it too."

"Really? How do you know that?"

"Because it says so in the Bible, that the demons will torment the people who don't have God's seal on their foreheads for five months. Those people will seek death but not find it" [Revelation 9:2-6].

Crystal's eyes grow wide. "You mean they will be like zombies?"

"Yeah, come to think of it, they will be like zombies." Brock turns and takes a step toward the river.

"No—wait! Where are you going? What if the zombies come here?"

Brock hollers over his shoulder, "If you see any zombies, just go hide in the spider hole and wait till I get back."

Crystal jumps out of her chair. "No! Wait for me! Don't leave me—"

Brock stops. "I was just kidding, Copperhead. There are no zombies around here."

"Do you promise?"

"Yes, I promise."

Crystal sits back down and relaxes her small frame into the chair. "So where are you going?"

"I'm going down the river. I'm going to see if I can find that old lady. Oh, and while I'm gone don't forget to fill up another bucket of acorns."

"Don't we have enough already?"

"No, there's never enough. We need to store up enough to get us through the winter. I'll be back this afternoon. Be sure to keep your eyes and ears open, and if you hear anyone go hide in the spider hole."

****

Alarmed, Brock drags the thirty-two-gallon trash container toward their camp. *Maybe Crystal did hear footsteps outside her tent that day.* He'd brushed it off as raccoons, but maybe she was right and did hear someone.

He'd stopped by JR's camp on the way back from searching for the old lady to get some more supplies when he'd discovered the tool box was gone. He searched the camp and found other items were missing, including the candle on the table.

Somebody took the tool box, but who?

He mulls over a list of suspects. *JR? Maybe he came back and found Crystal gone and grabbed a few things and left? Or the cop killer? That's a possibility. Someone murdered that cop and dumped his body in the river. Or maybe the old lady? Maybe she stumbled upon the camp and helped herself.*

His thoughts race a hundred miles an hour as he tugs the brown plastic over the bed of rocks.

He decides he's just paranoid and should relax and focus on things he needs to do like wash out the barrel and find another location more secure away from the river; he needs to build a sturdy shelter, a place where they can hide, possibly underground. He has so much to do and still hasn't found that old lady. Frustrated he wonders where she disappeared to. He spent most of the morning searching but still couldn't find her. He'd figured she had to live close by for even Crystal saw her.

Maybe something happened to her? Or. . .doubts cloud his brain. Maybe he'd misunderstood the riddle? Maybe he wasn't supposed to come to the Bear River after all?

****

"Crystal?" Brock shakes the fiberglass pole propping the tent up. "Crystal, are you in there?"

Silence.

He notices the small plastic bucket is gone.

She must still be picking up acorns. Good girl.

The hike down the canyon exhausted him, and he sits

down in the lawn chair. He fights the urge to sleep. After a while he gets up and putters around the camp, emptying the barrel then collecting firewood for the night. He wonders what they'll have for dinner. Maybe he'll dig into another MRE; he didn't have time to set the traps and is just too tired.

Why isn't Crystal back yet? She should be back by now.

Troubling thoughts harass him. *Maybe she got lost? No, she knows that if she gets lost to follow the canyon down to the river then follow the river back to camp.*

Maybe she fell and got hurt? A sick feeling deep down starts to rise.

Where is she?

"Dear Lord, please send Crystal back to camp unharmed."

"CRYSTAL!" he shouts as he climbs the slope behind their camp. "CRYSTAL!"

He tops the ridge. *Where is she? Maybe the cop killer stalked her? Or maybe JR came back and snatched her away? Or maybe she was attacked by a bear or a mountain lion?*

Sweat drips off his brow. He cups his hands over his mouth and shouts, "CRYSTAL!"

His legs carry him north along the ridge. "CRYSTAL!"

Lord, please help me find her.

"CRYSTAL!"

He hears a faint, whimpering cry from below.

Crystal? Brock's heart quickens.

He descends down the slope two steps at a time and finds Crystal lying on the ground holding her right foot, tears streaming down her face. A black flip-flop protrudes out of the pile of acorns that have spilled all over the ground.

"Crystal." Brock lets out his pent-up breath. "What

happened? Are you okay?"

"No. . . ," she moans. "A rattlesnake bit me. . .I was bit by a rattlesnake. . . ."

A rattlesnake? Brock gasps. *Stay calm,* he tells himself.

Her ankle is swollen more than twice its normal size, and red trickles from where the serpent sank its poisonous fangs.

"I–I was just walking back to camp. . . ." She tries to breathe. "I heard the rattles and looked down. Then it bit me. . .two times. . . ." She is sobbing.

Brock watches helplessly as the lethal dose of venom incapacitates Crystal. He can see her small 5-foot-4-inch body reacting to the toxins coursing through it.

He wants to scold her for not wearing her tennis shoes, but it's too late. What's done is done.

Fog blankets his mind. What should he do? Every book he'd read said to remain calm and go to the nearest health facility. The latest books said not to cut an X over the fang mark and suck out the venom as previously taught.

Bending over he takes her feeble arm and wraps it around his neck. Her skinny legs dangle as he hurries down the hill to the river.

"I'll have to go to town for help," he tells Crystal. "I don't care if they arrest me. I've got to get help!"

His breath is shallow as he stumbles over boulders and careens down the canyon. Frantic, he pushes ahead. *Lord, please help—please help me save her.*

He glances down at Crystal's face. Her lids are drooping, her skin ashen. Her ankle is the size of a basketball with large bloody, dark-colored blisters and bruising forming around the bite site.

Hurry! he urges himself on while the muscles in his back scream *Stop!* and his lungs plead with him to *get air!* It feels as if they're going to explode in his chest, but he ignores them and pushes forward, occasionally whispering words of comfort. "Don't worry, Crystal. I'm gonna get you some help. Hang in there, sweetie."

Crystal's cries turn into soft whimpers.

Brock's heart aches, and guilt invades him as he faces the reality that she may die. If only he hadn't sent her to gather more acorns. . . .

****

"Brock. . . ." Crystal's voice is brittle. "Brock. . .I'm thirsty. . . ."

"Okay, I'll get you some water."

Locating some shade below a pine, Brock sets Crystal gently on the soft needles and props her against the tree's trunk. But how can he get her some water?

He searches the river bed for a can or something, anything, but finds nothing. If he has to he'll carry her down to the water to drink; then he has an idea.

His fingers pull the cotton material over his head. The silver cross necklace Nicole had given him presses against his chest. He soaks the green T-shirt in the water and twists and squeezes it a few times before he saturates it again. He hurries over and kneels next to Crystal.

"Here—lay your head back and open your mouth."

Crystal closes her eyes and tilts her head backward.

Brock wrings the water into her mouth.

She sips noisily, like a puppy slurping its milk.

Brock wipes her face then returns to the river repeating the procedure until she closes her mouth and refuses any more water.

"Are you ready to go?" Brock's voice is urgent. "We have to keep moving. If we hurry we might get to the road before dark."

"No. . . ." Crystal says faintly. "I'm tired. . .I feel sick."

"But—"

Crystal leans over, and in one explosive moment her stomach empties all the water she'd just drunk.

Brock drops down beside her and cradles her head in his lap; he feels helpless as she deteriorates before his very eyes.

"Brock. . .I'm going to die, aren't I?"

Ignoring her question he strokes her head, fighting back tears. His throat is dry, and his heart aches. He hasn't felt anguish like this since his mother committed suicide.

Crystal shifts her head to look up at him, but her eyes stop at his chest. Her frail hand reaches out and clasps the silver cross.

"Brock." Crystal swallows hard, reaching for air. "Thank you. Thank you for finding me. . .if you hadn't found me I would've never known the truth about Jesus. . . ."

Brock stares straight ahead and continues to stroke her red locks. Her words replay in his head: *If you hadn't found me, I would've never known the truth about Jesus. . . ."*

Then Brock remembers the Lord's words: "Brock, one of My sheep is lost. I have chosen you to go and find her and bring her to Me."

Crystal? Was she the lost sheep?

The realization hits him like a bolt of lightning.

It was Crystal all along, not the old lady. Crystal was the lost sheep! How could he have been so blind? She was right there under his nose the whole time.

He is overcome by an intense feeling of relief mixed with joy; a giant burden rolls off him. Tears pour down his cheeks. He has this sudden urge to hold her and comfort her as a father comforts his child.

"Crystal." He pulls her to his chest and cradles her, resting his stubble chin on her head and holding her hand as he rocks her back and forth. His joy mixes with sadness then grief when he glances down at her ankle. The venom's digestive action has started to melt away the tissue near the wound.

Why, Lord? Why? he cries silently. *Why did she have to get bit? Why couldn't it have been me?*

Crystal squeezes Brock's hand weakly. He knows—this is the end. He holds her ragdoll body in his arms.

"Brock?" she murmurs. "Brock. . .do you see Him?" Her breath comes in puffs.

"No, Crystal, there's nobody there."

Crystal releases Brock's hand and tries to sit up. She reaches out as though she is reaching for someone.

"He's beautiful, Brock! I. . .I. . . ." One last gasp then her body falls limp against Brock's chest, her eyes still open.

"Crystal? No, Crystal. . .come back!"

Holding her tight he lets out a long anguished cry. He holds her lifeless body and brushes the hair out of her face, closing her eyes, then kisses her forehead.

Brock feels hollow inside as he continues to hold her, refusing to accept that her spirit has departed from her body. He weeps every last tear stored inside until he can weep no more.

He swipes at the tears on his face then gazes across to the white foaming river as it flows downstream as if nothing has happened.

The dropping sun signals that it's almost dark. It's too dangerous to hike back to camp; he'll have to stay the night and bury Crystal in the morning.

He gazes at Crystal's face; she looks as though she is sleeping.

Brock lays her gently on the ground then plants

another kiss on her brow.

The urge to survive fights against his weariness. He must pile up rocks and make a barrier, stacking branches to create a canopy to help protect him against the chilly night air. But he's too drained emotionally and physically; it will be easier to crawl under a rock and die.

The moon peeks over the tree tops as he places the last branch against the boulder and crawls inside his makeshift shelter; he chooses to survive.

Goose bumps rise and sore arms wrap over his chest trying to keep him warm as cold air envelops his body. His grieving soul cries out, *Why, Lord? Why? Why did Crystal have to die? Just when she finally accepted You. . . .*

His eyelids are heavy, and he struggles to stay awake. If he falls asleep he may wake to discover wild animals have stolen Crystal's corpse during the night. Eventually sleep overtakes him, and he falls into a deep dream state. . . .

Brock is sure he'd heard a growl. His mind goes to Crystal, lying cold and alone in the dark.

His heart pounds as he envisions a coyote dragging her body into the woods.

He feels for a stone; he's ready to defend Crystal in death as he defended her in life.

He scans the outside of his
shelter. A small breeze stirs the tree shadows making them waltz on the ground, but one shadow stands out from the others. It isn't dancing; it is huddled beside Crystal's body.

Staring at the shadow that is shaped like a hunchback man, Brock slowly stands to his feet.

"Hey, you!" Brock yells, raising his arm, gripping the rock. "Get away from her!"

The cowering creature turns a distorted head that protrudes from its winged shoulders. Beady eyes glare back at Brock under the grim light of the moon; it breathes in labored hisses. "She was mine!" The evil spirit unleashes its fury. "I conquered and owned her; then you snatched her from the fire like a burning stick."

Brock pulls his shoulders back and pushes his chest out. "The Lord rebuke you!"

The evil spirit hisses through double rows of fanged teeth. "I hate you! You will pay! She was mine—"

"In the name of Jesus leave!" Brock commands.

As Brock sleeps, thoughts and pictures continue to play out in his mind.

A silvery orb twirls across the black sky in a spiral wind then descends to earth and lands a few feet from Crystal's feet. The ball of light transforms into the likeness of a tall man; his white robe glistens, and his hair looks like spun gold.

The demon's face contorts in horror. It shields its eyes with its clawed hand.

"Be gone!" orders the tall being. A fiery beam of light emits from his mouth and penetrates the demon's scale-like body.

The serpentine creature lets out a piercing scream then stretches out its wings. In a split second it vanishes into the atmosphere.

The man turns to Brock. "Grace and peace be upon you from Him who is and who was and who is to come."

Brock drops to his knees, awed by the man's power and majesty.

"Stop!" he orders. "I am only a fellow servant like you. Worship only God Almighty!"

Brock stands, gazing in wonder at the bronze face of the angel of God. He gazes deep into his flaming blue eyes, somehow struck by a certain familiarity.

"You. . .you were the prison guard?"

Light gleams from the angel as he smiles. "Yes. And I was the bailiff who diverted you from worshipping the statue of the beast."

For a moment his thoughts return to Buddy when he told him that although Nicole was deaf some people claimed she could hear angels.

"Were you also the street prophet?"

"Yes. I was sent by Him who sits upon the throne and dwells and feeds His flock; like a good shepherd His sheep do not hunger or thirst or shed tears anymore for He leads them to living fountains of waters."

The angel raises his silken arm and points into the air.

The sky parts as the Red Sea did for the Israelites. Black waves roll away to reveal an image like a mirage of colors sitting on the clouds. The image enlarges, and Brock sees a multitude of people rejoicing and wearing white garments.

"Who are those people?"

"Those are the tribulation saints," the angel says. "They are before the throne of God and serve Him day and night in His temple."

Brock notices a man and woman hugging and embracing someone. Then he sees copper-colored hair.

"Crystal?!" he says excitedly under his breath.

"Yes!" The angel smiles.

"But who are the man and woman with her?"

"Those are her parents. They were martyred for their faith in Jesus. When they were here on earth they prayed continuously for their daughter who was kidnapped, never giving up hope."

Joy floods Brock as he watches the happy reunion.

"Rejoice," the angel tells Brock. "For you have found His sheep that was lost! Well done, my fellow servant, well done!"

If a man have an hundred sheep, and one of them be gone astray, doth he not leave the ninety and nine, and goeth into the mountains, and seeketh that which is gone astray? And if so be that he find it, verily I say unto you, he rejoiceth more of that sheep, than of the ninety and nine which went not astray. Even so it is not the will of your Father which is in heaven, that one of these little ones should perish.
Matthew 18:12-14

THE END